PRAISE FOR TEA HA

Tea Hacic is an MDMA-fueled Oscar Wilde with fake eyelashes and this book is a *Fear and Loathing* for the late Berlusconi-era; a deep walk of shame that tiptoes between a bewildering Bildungsroman and a fever dream of social climbing and social embarrassment.

— OLIVER KUPPER, EDITOR-IN-CHIEF OF
AUTRE MAGAZINE

A recollection of youth as seen through the dichotomy of control vs desperation, Americana vs. Milanese, luxury vs poverty and uppers vs downers.

— BJ PANDA BEAR AT FLAUNT MAGAZINE

Tea recounts with brutal honesty the period in which Milan officially became the Italian city that everyone hates and envies.

— VICE ITALY

Life of the Party is a good goddamn time.

— COLUMBIA JOURNAL

Reading *Life of the Party* is like drinking a coffee with Tea Hacic herself. Her light comes through the pages, her story becomes yours somehow. That's the power of storytelling."

— VANITY TEEN

Clever debut novel of fashion and nightlife, readers are introduced to Mia, an expat newly moved to Milan. The drugs, nightclubs, and men blur together into a seemingly nonstop, Fear and Loathing in Las Vegas-style fever dream as intense as it is dripping with style.

— PUBLISHERS' WEEKLY

It's as intoxicating as the best party you've ever been to...Hacic-Vlahovic has written one hell of a ride.

— THE BIG SMOKE

Hacic-Vlahovic's novel is so well-written and constructed.

— QUAILBELL MAGAZINE

LIFE OF THE PARTY is an unstoppable climax, made of strong but honest opinions that will make you question your past, present and your future...Tea gives us an unmatched depiction of some of the most meaningful contradictions that make us who we are.

— FRENCH FRIES MAGAZINE

LIFE OF THE PARTY

TEA HACIC-VLAHOVIC

CL◀SH

For Stefano

I see the world through rats' eyes

— BLACK FLAG

1. BELLA MERDA

Milan shouldn't be seen during the day. It's too ugly and not in a cool way. It's not a grungy music video or a teenage runaway. It's a woman waking up hung-over, looking in a mirror, and screaming because she lost all her collagen overnight.

It's pathetic because it wishes it weren't ugly.

"E' brutalismo?" I ask the church.

"No, solo brutto," the gargoyles answer.

So the Duomo is full on weekends.

People need to do something in the daylight but can't bear the sight of their own neighborhoods. Saturday and Sunday, they pour out of trams and walk around in circles. They fill up H&M and ZARA and shops that exist in every city on earth. I know because I do the same thing. I sit on the Duomo steps and light a cigarette.

The pigeons crowd around me.

"Hey dudes, what's up?"

An albino pigeon with a runny eye and a grey pigeon with a missing toe are fighting over the butt of a cigarette.

"Eating trash and getting stepped on, you?"

"Same," I shrug.

The pigeons are pimped out by immigrants. Tourists pay a couple euros to be covered in seeds, provided by the immigrants, who are then paid to take polaroid pictures of the tourists covered in pigeons eating the seeds. As soon as the picture is taken, the tourists scream and flap their arms around, tossing the pigeons away. "Disgusting!" they yell, as the pigeons run for their lives, confused and hurt by the ordeal.

I hate people.

And I don't get the big deal about the Duomo. Sure, I get dizzy when I see it from a taxi window. And when I look at it close-up I want to cry. But I always want to cry, so that doesn't mean anything. They never let me inside the Duomo because I was dressed too slutty. And I can guess it doesn't have WI-FI.

I doubt it has good bathrooms either.

A good bathroom has it all. A full toilet with a sturdy seat. Not a bare shell and definitely not a "squat." A hole in the ground, can you imagine? I'd rather crap my pants! A good bathroom also has air conditioning, plenty of toilet paper and a large, well-lit mirror. I need to check my eyeliner *and* my thigh gap, thanks.

The best bathrooms in Milan are at: Straf Bar, LaRinascente and Santa Tecla.

The worst bathrooms in Milan are at: Bar Cuore, Atomic, and my apartment.

My WC is cramped and cold, even in the summer. The air is that of a basement in some Soviet building full of landmines and mold. One light bulb hangs overhead, threatening me with its glow. The shadows it creates on my face make me look like a witch that eats babies. (Wrong: I'm vegetarian!) The toilet seat has a screw loose, the shower leaks, the curtain is moldy. The mirror is tiny and useless. I'm insulted someone put it there at all. I have to do my makeup in the hallway and dye my hair in the kitchen. People look down on me from the sidewalk. The windows don't shut completely. It's an open invitation for kidnapping, if anyone would want me. The ceiling is so low I high-five it when I shave my armpits.

I share the loft with Maria. She's a journalist my age from Liguria. I don't know where Liguria is, but I think it's in the North. Maria's too icy to be Southern. I met her at a party in some guy's loft. She ended up kissing my date and I ended up kissing hers. Then we ended up leaving together. I told her I needed a place and she told me she needed a roommate. We split the rent, which is 700 euros a month. Maria dropped out of school to work full time for an online fashion magazine. "It's the first one in Italy," she claims. I hate to tell her there's no future in online publishing. Only an idiot would stop buying paper magazines! We are bonded by our empty pockets and stomachs. The latter is a choice. We both have eating disorders we refuse to admit to. I've had mine since I was thirteen.

One morning I was eating SPECIAL K and reading the back of the box.

"LOSE SIX POUNDS IN TWO WEEKS WITH THE SPECIAL K DIET"

The box suggested I eat one bowl of SPECIAL K for breakfast, another bowl for lunch and then a "smart" dinner. I had never considered my weight before that summer, when my aunt told me my ass was too big for boys to like me. I did the diet and lost six pounds. It felt like magic, having control over my body. Soon "two bowls of cereal + dinner" turned into "two apples + dinner" and then "just dinner." Once I'd mastered that, I would allow only a breakfast pastry or bowl of oatmeal to enter me each day. Then, I mustered the strength to go liquid.

Every day I would wake up and think, "should I weigh myself or have a good day?" Then I would have a bad day. A soy cappuccino or prune juice were considered meals. By the time I was seventeen I was a hardcore anorexic. Black coffee and sugar-free candies were my source of nutrients. I was doing great - until I ended up in the hospital with a kidney disorder. My body didn't have the strength to deal with a simple urinary tract infection (my boyfriend never washed his hands) so she took the opportunity to shut down and get a hospital vacation. Touché. The whole ordeal felt glamorous; I was finally like the subject of a tragic movie we'd see in school as kids. *Women: They Suffer Because They're Stupid!* The most irritating part was how my friends and family reacted. Che drama. I guess they were all jealous of how skinny I was.

I didn't want to die yet (I had to see how *The OC* would end) so I introduced myself back to food, slowly, mixed with handfuls of laxatives and a lot of "chewing and spitting." Now my metabolism is more fucked than a girl at mens' fashion week. I'm bloated and soft, even though I only consume like a thousand calories daily. Most of that comes from alcohol. Can you believe I put in all those years of effort, just to become a 22-year-old with that same stupid thirteen year old body? I wish the infection had killed me! (The last season of *The OC* wasn't even worth living for). Sometimes I consider trying to eat normally but then what would be special about me?

Watching Maria struggle with food is annoying. She's not bulimic or anorexic anymore, she's in recovery, which is worse. Like me, she skips meals daily and lies about how much she ate when nobody asked in the first place. It makes me feel embarrassed about my own issues, so I resent her for that. It's like when we were all shooting up heroin in North Carolina and I said to my boyfriend, "look how gross Josh looks when he nods-out" and my boyfriend said, "that's how you look when you nod-out."

It's a blessing that Maria and I can't afford to go to restaurants. I'd hate to see us try to maneuver our way out of a full meal. We do have aperitivo often. Mostly on the Naviglio. Our favorite spot is called Luca and Andrea. There we pack plastic plates full of antipasti and potato chips. Then, we theatrically move stuff around and eat only the low-calorie trimmings: tomatoes, olives, pickles and onions. We pretend for each other the way we would with our parents. Acting normal is an art we've mastered over the years—why waste it?

At home we live off cornflakes and instant coffee. I stock the fridge with Tavernello, a boxed wine that costs one euro. Half liters are fifty cents and I pack them into my purse when I can't afford cocktails. Which is almost every night.

Sometimes I come home from a party before dawn, meaning I didn't score drugs or a body. If Maria is still up writing, and she usually is, we watch *Sex and the City* dubbed in Italian. She pulls out a hidden jar of Nutella that we eat with a spoon. It's a little tradition that sets my self-hatred dial to MAXIMUM.

Maria says she was once a celebrated gymnast but I can't picture it. She's got the looks for it but no grace. She's clumsy. She leaves piles of dirty clothes around and never washes her dishes. A pyramid of cups with dried cornflakes and orzo powder form in the sink. She sets alarms at ten minute intervals from 6:00 to 7:00 and sleeps through all of them. I can't sleep through anything, so I end up bitterly getting up to shake her awake. She's usually passed out on the couch fully clothed with the TV on mute. It's a self-harm thing. As a teenager I did the same thing. I empathize with her and love her, but her sadness makes mine worse.

Sometimes she pisses me off. Once she stole a pair of tights from my dresser. Otherwise they disappeared on their own and that's impossible. I cherish my tights and when they rip I mourn all day. Until recently I slept in tights. For years I couldn't stand to feel my legs touching, even when laying down. I'm glad I can sleep naked now (I had to learn once I started sleeping with strangers). But I never wear pants so if I don't have clean tights in the winter I'm screwed. When I've only got twenty euros left over a weekend I can get a couple tram tickets, a pack of cigarettes and a few aperitivos. If I rip a pair of tights you know where the money goes. When I'm broke I rely on my charm to get drinks and smokes and that only brings trouble.

Maria gets weird when I talk about boys. I thought she might be gay like my last roommate, but I've determined she isn't. She's just delusional. The woman actually believes that a guy should talk to her first. What universe does she think we're in? I told her that if I waited for boys to talk to me I'd still be a virgin. She's prettier than me so I don't know what her problem is. Things could be easy for her. A natural blonde with green eyes and a button nose. She looks like a drawing of a girl on a bar of Swedish chocolate. Still, she's sour, over something. When she found out I was dating a Biker and a Buddhist at the same time she didn't speak to me all day.

To be fair, she was judgmental in that case because she knew how I met the Biker. This time last year, the two of us were waiting for a tram in 24 Maggio, when a Biker stopped at the red light. I couldn't see his face because he was wearing a blackout helmet. But he had "hot energy." He was like Daft Punk with a good body. I could tell he was checking me out. I can't explain how, but there were witches in my family so I've inherited some senses. The Biker called me over and told me to write down his number.

Maria stared me down the whole time, scandalized. I came back to her, beaming. I still hadn't seen his face.

"Are you crazy?"

"Yeah, why?"

I called him the next day. We met at the Colonne in Ticinese. I was half an hour early, as usual. I wore a black nylon dress. He showed up in leather and denim and turned out to be a total babe. Like, imagine one of those naked statues in

Rome or whatever—imagine if it came alive, put on an outfit from DIESEL and started walking beside you, with those muscles and dimples and curls. The only difference between him and those Roman statues is that he has a big dick. I found out that night. First, we had dinner at McDonald's, where he ate two Big Macs and I drank diet coke. Then he took me to his place on his motorcycle(!). He had one of those apartments that exist only in the realm of college boys. The kind of dirty that takes years to make. The next day he fed me cookies and milk.

I barely spoke Italian then so it was hard for me to tell if a guy was cool or *"testa di cazzo."* I really liked my Biker so I preferred not to find out. We barely communicated at all but we couldn't get enough of each other. It never got awkward not talking since he kept me busy, riding his bike or his body. By winter he found out about the Buddhist and then the Buddhist found out about him.

2. SHEENA IS A PARASITE

Our apartment is the only one of its kind in our building. It's ground level, under the stairs. The front door looks too small to walk through. It used to belong to housekeeping, back in the medieval times, or 1950's, or whatever. Everyone in our building is a rabbi or socialite or a private school kid draped in Gucci. Only Maria and I are cheap tramps. She isn't a tramp, she's just a bitch. But here a girl is considered bad if she lives with a girl who is. Especially if the bad girl is foreign. They say Croatians come to Italy to steal husbands. But I'm not so predictable. I'm also American. I could steal anything.

We live in Corso Plebisciti, close to Plastic Club and nothing else. I can walk there in ten minutes. Otherwise I've got the most basic block. A grocery store, a kebab place and a pub that intended to be Irish but didn't have the commitment to see it through.

Once I tried to "explore my neighborhood" and found a park. The trees were emaciated and the ground was grey and filthy. No kids around, thank god, just a few junkies. I sat on a bench and read an entire novel, about a Chinese girl who moved to Beijing from the countryside to become an actress.

She didn't make it as an actress. It made me so lonely I swore I'd never look at or breathe the air of that park again. So I spend all my time taking buses and trams. They take ten times longer than the Metro but I don't like being underground. The rats don't want us down there.

My school, work and current boyfriend are across town, in Porta Genova. I carry an oversized purse around. It's a used black nylon Longchamp with leather straps and it's grotesque. It's filled with underwear, tights, makeup, a toothbrush and my laptop. This way I can stay away from home for days—crashing with boys, friends, or not crashing.

The atmosphere that Maria and I create at our place is too dense. The air is thick with our dreams. We both need urgently to bury who we are and become someone less pitiful. Our collective ambition is too vast for the walls to contain. There is no door in the loft to divide our energy. We pushed our beds to opposite ends of the floor but you can't invent space that ain't there. She has the place to herself a few nights a week. She needs peace to write her articles but I can become who I need to be at a party.

My boyfriend says my apartment is the perfect place for a puttana. Milanese buildings are complicated, with gates, buzzers, doormen and old widows spying from their balconies. I've got easy access and privacy. Nobody cared about housekeeping so nobody cares about me. Men can sneak in and out easily. This season I've had dozens undetected by neighbors. One even used the window. I have lots of boys but only one I call my boyfriend—secretly. He wouldn't like it if he knew, and neither would his wife.

I always end up in other people's relationships.

When I got here two years ago, I became obsessed with my landlord. He was my first "Real Man" if there is such a thing. My first non-teenage junkie, at least. His features were from another time, like someone your grandma would show you in an old picture and say, "he was the most handsome boy in town but one day he coughed and the next day he died."

He wore tailored clothes with nice fabric. I wanted to kiss his D&G belt. He ran a leather factory in the basement of our building but always cruised around the dorms to show the stupid Americans (me) how to use wooden shutters or turn on a gas stove. After school I'd lay in bed and agonize over the thought of him being so close.

I was sharing a dorm with a lesbian named Lindsay. We were cool at first, she loved me because I let her drag me to lesbian bars. But when I found a girl before she did she stopped inviting me. Which is good because those bars didn't play the kind of music I like. I only went out with that one girl because she spoke English. She was furious when I told her, "I'm not gay but we can still kiss sometimes." I broke this news when she brought a rose to my place in the middle of the night. She cried and threw the flower on the ground. Women are embarrassing.

Anyway, Lindsay and I shared a washing machine that hardly worked. I'd call Silvio up to fix it. I made him come over every day. All I thought about at school was what I'd do if he let me touch him. Every day I'd come up with a complicated plan leading to a complex fantasy about him coming upstairs and ravishing me! Then he'd come for real and I'd chicken out and wash clean clothes because he fixed the machine. He'd leave and I'd chain smoke on the balcony with blue balls. Eventually he got the hint, which was a godsend, since I was *this close* to jumping off my balcony or calling my lesbian ex.

"Your washing machine works perfectly," Silvio said, grabbing the top of the door frame and leaning over me.

"I know." I looked up at him, leaning back on the washing machine.

"So why do you call me here every day?" He reached out and tugged on my hair.

"Why do you think?"

He laughed and kissed me, out of pity. That night he took me out for overflowing, overpriced cocktails near the Castello. He told me about parties I'd never be caught dead at —glitzy stuff for aspiring escorts and entrepreneurs. Hollywood, Old Fashioned and The Club. He kept laughing at me and I couldn't figure out why. Back then I didn't know I was funny. He stopped his sports car on the side of the street when I needed to puke.

"Baby! What happened?"

"Evry cocktel haz 200 calorees."

"What?"

"I skip dinnr wen I drnk."

He took me to bed in the penthouse of a Corso Como skyscraper. He had heated floors and a drawer full of Armani basics. I know because he opened it to give me a white shirt to sleep in. Later my nose bled on it *and* his bed and he didn't accuse me of being a cokehead! He just changed the sheets. He had an extra set. Che riccanza. My last boyfriend slept on a bare mattress. Che squallore. In the morning he dropped me off across the street from my dorm.

"Wait a few minutes before walking home."

"Why?"

"We can't go inside together."

"Because you're my landlord?"

"Sure, baby."

We went out every night from summer till winter. My summer outfits stayed the same but I added tights and a fur coat from the vintage market. I've always been vegetarian but I tried it on "for fun" and heard a girl behind me say, "if you don't get it I will" so I had to. The animal's spirit is safer in my hands. Also I shaved my head that fall and Silvio hated it!

"Baby what did you do?"

"Cool, right?" I rubbed my head like velvet.

"Now I *really* hide you. Ha!"

"Ha!...wait, *huh?*"

My obsession waned the better I got to know him. I hated myself for caring about the fact that he was so...normal. I can get past bad taste and listening to the radio, but if you aren't even punk *inside*...well, it's hard to explain. But I was having fun. I was fancying myself becoming his girlfriend. Why not? I'd love to be some lady in a red dress, laughing at a standing dinner. Champagne glass in one hand and lies in another. I wanted to get to know him better, seeing as how I'd eventually move in with him. I had to see this thing through for the other girls in the dorms who were so jealous of me they could *die*. Thanks to my unabashed and unabridged stories they all got to have him.

I dug through his stuff while he showered. He had Ibiza summer playlists, "best of" dance music and Euro Trash compilations from the AutoGrill. I was horrified. But what I saw next was worse. Photo albums full of pictures of him with a fancy blonde. On boats and stuff. With horses!

"Who's this? Your sister?"

"No baby. My fiancé."

It used to drive me crazy (good) to be called baby. But I've learned that Italian men only call you that when they don't remember your name. When my boyfriend calls me my name it electrocutes me to death. But he only does when he's mad.

"Mia, you're so loose today."

My boyfriend is sticking a beer bottle in me while I lay on the floor.

"Yeah I banged two guys last night."

Last night he called me from outside my apartment. He was in a car, wasted, waiting for me. He gets nasty when he's drunk. I was glad I couldn't see the look on his face when he slurred into the phone. I told him I was across town with my friends. He demanded I come anyway. I didn't have the cab fare. I was pissed that he thought I would drop everything for him! And more pissed that...I wanted to. So I stayed with my friends and slept with them both to make some kind of point.

3. ODIO TUTTI

Last year I worked in a menswear showroom, or as we call it in the industry, a cesspool for boy toys. My job was to dress and undress them. My job was also to: organize the inventory, arrange meetings, vacuum the floors, clean the toilet, steam the suits, iron the shirts, run errands, take out trash, fetch lunch, make coffee, pour champagne, serve the clients, assist the clients, read their minds, feed their egos and get bullied by my bosses. I had three of them. The two designers—a gay couple—and the head designer's sister. She's the sales representative and a pain in my ass.

Her favorite part of the day was the morning. She'd come in at 8:00 and expect her breakfast to be served instantly, on the black polished (tacky) desk in the middle of the showroom. Once seated, she'd change into black Balenciaga heels, which she carries in a purse, because she's a pussy and can't walk in them. I walk in high heels every day—like, *actually* walk—she takes taxis everywhere! I can't fathom being so pathetic. Anyway, opening hour was her favorite part of the day because it's the part when her and I were alone and she could make fun of me while I cleaned. (She'd make fun of me all day but its most effective when I'm cleaning).

"MIA! Come!" Her shrill voice stabbed my hung-over head.

I put down the vacuum and ran. "Yes?"

"Is that a Saks Fifth shopping bag?" she pointed to my purse, on the floor.

"*Off* Saks Fifth! The outlet in North Carolina."

"I didn't know they had an outlet..."

"Yeah! I get all my nice stuff there."

"Really?" she giggled. "I've never seen you wear nice stuff."

"Well—"

"Why do you carry this shopping bag?"

"I use it as a purse."

"Oh!" she gasped, put a hand on her chest. "You poor thing. I have some old designer bags laying around...maybe I could lend you one."

"Really?"

"Yeah but...I just can't picture you with it."

I told my mom what happened and she sent me her old Longchamp purse in the mail. My boss's bullying stung but it never stuck to me for long. I'd hate to be her. She's fat and over thirty. She's a bully, the old-fashioned kind. She doesn't see irony in being bitchy, like gay men do. She just...*is mean* and thinks that's a personality. Some people shouldn't be themselves. Her brother is an ass, too. He told me that him and his sister used to buy cheap clothes and sew designer labels on them and then sell the pieces to their "poor" class-mates. Scum! But they look good on my resume.

"Mia, what the hell are those?" my boss looked at me like I dragged dog shit onto the table.

"Two glasses of wine. Why?" I put down a glass in front of her and another in front of the Russian client. He was built like a mountain. His suits were always bursting at the seams.

"They're filled to the brim! You think we're alcoholics?" my boss asked defensively, patting the Russian client on the shoulder.

"No. I mean, what?"

"Have you never ordered a glass of wine before?"

I thought about it. No, I haven't ever ordered a glass of wine before. I've only poured them at home or seen my friends pour them...we usually fill them up to the top. I can't possibly imagine why anyone would do otherwise.

My boss tapped the glass near the bottom. "This is where you pour. No more. Now go downstairs and fix it."

I reached for the glasses but the Russian client stopped me.

"Don't waste wine. I can drink it." He winked at me. I went back to the kitchen. The kitchen is beneath the dressing room, in the basement. The basement is cement. It was always wet and cold and stinking. I spent hours down there. I wondered if Europeans have asbestos and poured myself a glass of wine, to the top.

I came in five days a week from 8:00 to 20:00. During fashion week and the sales season that followed, it became seven days a week from 8:00 to 22:00. I told them I had night classes I was missing but they didn't care. I didn't either.

My colleague was this South Korean girl that was built like a Barbie. Tall, thin, with big boobs, long hair, a perfect complexion, "dick sucking" lips...so unfair. I hated looking at her. I knew her from the dorms. We were in the same study abroad program. When all the other kids went home after a semester, back to their "real" lives, only Handley and I stayed behind. I was running from heroin and three boys who shared me like we shared needles. I wonder what dark story she left behind but she never told me. She's a cunt.

Handley wore fur. The fresh kind. Fur that had to live in cages. I don't know why she worked with me because she didn't need the money. I asked her how much her furry Fendi boots cost. She said "a lot." I asked her how many pairs of shoes she had. She started to count in her head and after a minute, said, "I don't know." Later she asked me how many guys I've slept with. I started to count in my head and after a minute, said, "I don't know."

The bosses joked that they "pay me in flesh." They didn't know the half of it. Their showroom was just a front for my dating service. Product: unlimited. Clients: just me! You don't need to be hot to get a model. You just have to be cool. A French model I went out with described me as "a young Lydia Lunch." And he was being generous. The really pretty girls I know don't have as much fun as me because they love themselves. Loving yourself gets in the way of having fun. So if you're ugly remember: being hot isn't cool but being cool is hot!

My boyfriend knows this. That's why he likes me and why I like him. He's the furthest thing from hot. I mean, he has a fit body and a masculine face but...he only wears active wear in shades of ugly. He has no music taste that I know of. And he's the one driving me mad? Humiliating me on the daily? Debasing me in ways I never knew possible? And he's not even mine, what a joke. I stare at him while he drinks his cocktail. He's got the hairiest hands.

"People who think sex is about good bodies aren't having real sex," he says.

"What do you mean?" I get out of my head and look around at the bodies. He took me to a swinger's club tonight. But we aren't having sex.

"I wish I were fatter so when I fuck you, you could feel me everywhere."

"Oh I feel you!" I gulp my martini and hope he shuts up.

"You'd look great with a leash."

"Yeah, well, the problem with sex toys is someone has to pay for them."

We've been meeting at swinger's clubs lately because our usual bar, PRAVDA, is becoming off-limits. Everyone and their mom has seen us there together. He fingered me at

PRAVDA once, on the red couches. People were all around us when he pushed my leotard aside and put a finger in my butt. It's a special place for us. When he leaves his wife I'll throw us a big party there. Guest list: all of our exes. A sea of suckers, flooding the streets.

Every day the models came in stinking. They never showered in their lives. They showed up in baggy sweatpants, with the knees stretched out like postpartum bellies. Bony hands gripping greasy bags of focaccia from the bakery. They stained all of the white shirts in oil. They were just kids, from sad countries in really cold places or really hot places. "For our mannequins!" My boss would yell, shoving clothes at us without eye contact. She dehumanized the models because she knew she had no chance with them.

I took good care of my boys. I dressed them up with love. I imagined I was getting them ready for something special, like graduation, a job interview or jail. When I'd zip their pants up and tuck their shirt into it, they knew. They'd get hard when I put on their shoes. By the time the first shift was over we'd have a date. They took me to "model apartments" north of Loreto, where dozens of them slept together, packed like sardines in bunk beds. Frozen pizzas, ashtrays and energy drinks. Socks filled with semen. Weekly allowances, bookers who blew them, agents who stole from them. I was their big sister. I gave them what they missed from home. I'd clean up their place before leaving.

Men feel safe in their muck. My boyfriend's place is filthier than a male model's. He has a maid come once a week but her efforts are futile. Some guys never grow out of it. I think he's being as gross as possible while he still can. His wife called while I laid with him in bed. His voice is different with her. He sounds small. While he talked, I coughed, by accident. (I'm pretty sure it was accident). He covered my mouth, panicked. I heard her ask, "what was that?" He told her, "I'm sick." I'm in big trouble.

"I'll only fuck you once a month so you don't get spoiled."

We're wasted, leaving a noise concert in a basement. He takes me to events neither of us enjoy, just to show off his collection of contacts.

"Fine! Every other day of the month I'll fuck someone else!" I yell.

He grabs my shirt and, with both hands, rips it down the middle, in the middle of the street. Everyone watches me watching him walk away and get into a taxi. What's with him and ripping shirts? It's un-wearable now. The PRAVDA shirt he bought for me on one of our first dates. I take it off and stand in my bra. As I watch him drive off, I vow to never see or speak to him ever again.

He texts me later and I come over. He ties me under the dinner table. He takes advantage of my anxiety. I don't like what he's into but I do it because otherwise he wouldn't want me.

"I don't need a girlfriend, I need a slave."

Those words haunt me. But being submissive is easy. It's the easiest thing in the world. You just don't have to do anything. And I'm good at that. I can stop doing whatever you want. Name something and I'll stop it: studying, eating, sleeping, moving, breathing, living. The only thing I can't stop is being stupid.

Handley doesn't date the showroom models. She already has a model boyfriend who is "established," or in other words, unemployed. One night she showed up at my place when I was on my way out. She was a crying mess, like a cat that went through a heavy cycle in a washing machine. She carried comically large Louis Vuitton luggage and held coats and bags in her arms. She looked incredible.

"He beat me up."

"What! Who?"

"My boyfriend."

"Oh my god! I'm so sorry." I hoped I sounded sincere. I was, I think.

"Can you bring my bags in?"

"Oh. Yeah."

She watched me pull her belongings inside.

"Can I sleep here?"

She looked at Maria on the couch. Maria looked at her.

"Of course! You've got it!" I said. Maria sighed and she got off her favorite cushion. She shuffled upstairs with her laptop.

"Thanks." Handley laid down on the Ikea sofa. Suddenly it looked expensive.

"Are you OK?" I asked her.

"I'm hungry," she said.

"Oh. I don't have much here." I pretended to shuffle through my kitchen, knowing very well exactly how many flakes of cereal there were.

"It's OK. You can order something!" she yelled from the sofa.

"Oh! Ok...Like pizza?"

"I'm sick of pizza. What about sushi?"

The nerve of this girl.

There's nothing I hate more in this world than watching a naturally skinny girl eat...but doing it on my tab? You've got to be kidding me! She stayed on the couch all night but stayed awake the whole time, texting. She went back to her boyfriend's place the next morning. She'd rather live with an abusive boyfriend than Maria and me! I don't blame her.

I had to pay for her taxi. I haven't taken a taxi in weeks! At work that day I asked her about what happened and she pretended not to hear. Only rich people don't consider giving back money. That whole week sucked for me.

Every month or so my bosses switched the showroom boys for new ones. Great way to avoid saying "bye" or "you gave me chlamydia." The models came and went but the clients remained. This French buyer with black hair and blue eyes drove me crazy for several seasons. One day when my boss stepped out he finally asked me out.

Him and his dad own a shop in LA and they get the tackiest clothes. Whenever they got an appointment my boss made me dig through the basement. I'd rummage through bins filled with dust, rags and trash, on a mission to find drycleaning bags containing the cursed items: suits covered in sequins and leather studded with Swarovski. Pieces that remained locked in their tombs until the infamously tasteless Russian buyers descended from their thrones. Anyway. This French buyer, Cecil, wore ridiculous sneakers and shredded jeans and shirts with collars that drooped to his belly. Mr. Sleaze. He was in his late thirties and you could tell he was dirty. He smelled like an orgy and smiled at me like he just stole my wallet. Not to be corny, but looking into his eyes made my vagina commit suicide.

He took me to a restaurant in Galleria Vittorio Emanuele. Every dish was a month's rent. His dad came with us. He ordered octopus.

"You want some octopus?"

"No, thank you," I replied politely. I should have told him the octopus he was eating was probably smarter than him.

"Why not?" he asked me, slurping a tentacle.

"I'm saving room," I said. "For whatever your son is packing."

Cecil insulted me in French while he had me in his hotel room, dragging me from the bed to the bathroom floor. Then he tried to drown me in the tub, then he tried to drown me in the sink, then he almost drowned me in the toilet. When men are violent in bed it's because they don't know how to be good in bed. They distract you from how boring they are with the pain. Or they try to! *I'm so bored I could die, kill me daddy!* Being a woman is embarrassing but being a man is pathetic.

A buyer from Dubai had apartments all over Milan and shops who knows where. He always wore white. He was handsome but short and therefore evil. I guess he's killed a dozen people. Once he had a big fight with my bosses and said he'd never come back. I smoked a cigarette outside to avoid hearing them yelling. He came out onto the sidewalk, fuming.

"You're the best thing in this showroom!"

"I agree."

"I'll miss seeing you."

"Sucks for you."

"Do you like working here?"

"It's my dream come true."

"Do you need more money?"

"What do you think?"

He made me meet him in Buenos Aires for a "job opportunity." He picked me up on the street in velvet slippers. His apartment was decorated like Scarface's place. Versace Home Collection. I sat at a baroque table while he made tea.

"You'll write emails for me."

"You can't write your own emails?"

"I'll pay you 50 euros for each."

"Jesus Christ."

"I talk. You type."

I transcribed stuff I didn't understand. It was something shady. Anyone living in Milan from Dubai is shady. When we were done, he told me to take a bath. He prepared the water, then sat on the toilet and told me to get in. He watched me take my clothes off. I folded them on the sink. Then he left the bathroom and closed the door behind him. In half an hour the water got cold. He yelled from the bedroom.

"ARE YOU COMING?"

I yelled back. "I THOUGHT YOU WERE COMING!?"

"I'M WAITING FOR YOU IN BED!"

What in the hell.

He was laying on lush white blankets, arms out like Jesus. His boner stood taller than him. Who knows how long he held that pose.

While we did it he watched himself in the mirror. "Look how sexy you are!" He kept saying. But he didn't see me. And I can't stand the word "sexy." When it was done, he paid me. That whole summer I'd come over, write his emails and drink his tea. He didn't drink alcohol which blew my mind and made me hate his religion. I learned to have a few drinks before coming over. Then I'd take a bath, sleep with him and get paid. I made the baths take as long as possible.

I'd have incriminating dirt on him if I understood the emails. They seemed like arguments involving bribes or blackmail (...what's the difference?). Eventually six emails per night turned into three which turned into one which turned into none. But he still invited me over. That didn't work for me because the sex, like most sex, was bad. The first few nights were worth it, just for the bath, a new luxury. If only I could end it there. But, alas. We all know that sleeping with a guy is easier than trying not to.

It got too hot in town to take trams to Porta Venezia. Screw it! Showers are fine too. I called to say I'd be his secretary but "no more funny business!" I said call me *only* when you've got emails to write and let's *only* meet in public. He lost his mind completely. His brain boiled like his goddamn tea kettle.

He parked his car in front of my apartment and left threatening voicemails. "Come out and I'll kill you!" Bitch, I dare you. Having to turn my phone off bothered me more than having to leave my flat. He didn't know I had my Big Ugly Purse. I could disappear forever!

Eventually he did, too.

Milanese fog stabs you in the heart and rots your bones. I bring bags of brioches around for my birds. They're shivering in the park, waiting for it all to end: winter or their lives, whatever comes first. The romance. My little poets. If whatever I'm trying to do in fashion doesn't work out (and I guarantee that it won't) I can become "that lady on the bench covered in feathers." I'll be famous in my way.

"What's up, pigeons?"

"Freezing our asses off, you?"

A guy pigeon is trying desperately to bang a girl pigeon. She's not interested.

"Same."

"Did you cry today?"

The guy pigeon won't give up. Eventually the girl pigeon gives *it* up just to make him stop bugging her.

"No. But I will on the way home!"

Crying feels better than sex. At least I get a release. I'm not some kind of psychopath. I just can't cum with anyone and it drives me crazy. I've collected so much data, loads of experience, countless pregnancy tests and STD checks, for what? It's unfair that some virgin can do missionary and have a mind-blowing orgasm while I've got to embark on a *Lord of the Rings* quest just to feel...anything. My boyfriend doesn't do it for me either but at least he makes me cry more than anyone.

Sometimes I worry how far I'll go in hopes of feeling something. Some nights I walk around aimlessly, daring men to follow me. Sometimes they do and we end up screwing in the bushes or on a bench. I avoid getting inside their cars because, as a Sagittarius, I don't like being trapped. But nothing is really scary when you realize that anything *scary* is just a feeling you don't like. Being beaten up or walking in heels are just unpleasant sensations. And complaining about stuff is pointless because nothing is fair. Some girls can eat whatever they want and have legs that won't even touch if they cross them. Some girls have purses that aren't shopping bags.

At least I'm funny.

"At least you've got all your toes!"

The pigeons scuttle away and I catch a tram home.

It's Tuesday night and the party week has started.

4. CUNT CLUB

My weekly party schedule is as follows:

Tuesday: ROCKET

Rocket is an indie venue where everyone has asymmetrical haircuts, skinny jeans and a coke problem. They play the Yeah Yeah Yeahs and The Horrors, stuff like that. Downstairs there's a stage and bands put on shows sometimes. But I prefer when it's just a DJ so I can have more space to dance. Attention, give it to me! Lots of gorgeous boys come here but they aren't interested in hooking up. They are dedicated to their aesthetic, which I admire, from a distance.

Wednesday: CUNT CLUB

Cuore is a retro bar in Ticinese. The hottest dudes I've ever seen in my life run a party there called CUNT CLUB. Their names are Frank and Magro. Their bodies are so thin they could snap in half any second and their hair is so big it has its own gravitational pull. They DJ and sell drugs too. I always request "Human Fly" and "Psycho Killer" and they always play it for me. I'd die to sleep with one of them or both of them but they only sleep with socialites. Sometimes I show up too early to the party and nobody is there so I sit at the Colonne di San Lorenzo and talk to the hash dealers from Morocco. They treat me nicer than anyone else in town.

Thursday: BRUTTOPOSSE

There's a Spanish restaurant across the street from my school, on the Naviglio. To the left, down the stairs, there's a space as big as your grandma's living room. On Thursday nights, all the ultra-literate "media people" show up and play hip-hop. It's not my style but I always have fun. The first few hours of the night everyone just stands around staring at each other. "I hear he works for VICE," every girl says while pointing to any man in glasses. Everyone's desperate for drugs, dick or a day job. By 1:00 people either get what they want or don't and go downstairs to dance. They get sweaty as hell and the place smells like sewage by 2:00, then closes. These sisters are always there, identical twin girls who could be models but choose not to because they prefer to be artistic or something. I don't know. They either hate me or like me and I can't tell because we always see each other but always refuse to talk to each other. I saw Chloe Sevigny there one night. It was one of those moments when I thought, "I'm in the right place, pushing myself towards the right future." Then I made the mistake of also thinking, "she will love me, I should talk to her." I shudder to think of it now. Luckily she never came back.

Friday: PUNKS WEAR PRADA

Brit pop, poseurs and fashion people who go to the gym. It's at this club called Santa Tecla, right by the Duomo. When the club isn't hosting *PWP* it's hosting mafia meetings. This is the

best place to pick up models. I discovered they've got one of
the best bathrooms in town by spending an hour in it with a
cover boy named Isaac. We would have stayed in there all
night if a hundred girls weren't kicking the door in to take
coke dumps. That night I arrived with one of my showroom
boys, from Brazil, but I left him as soon as I saw Isaac
standing in line at the bar. I'd never done something so mean
but if you'd seen him you would have too! He shoved his
fingers in my mouth. One of them had the name of his girlfriend tattooed on it. We're still in touch.

Saturday: PINK IS PUNK

This party gets packed with local celebrities. Pretentious elec-
tronic music and fashion people who wouldn't step foot in a
gym to save their lives. The bathroom is a marketplace for
drugs. I always blackout when I go here so I can't really tell
you much about it. It's dark. Once I accidentally did ketamine
(I thought it was coke— sue me) and went into a deep K-Hole.
I woke up that morning on the sidewalk, without my coat on
my back and with a half-eaten sandwich in my hand. Which
pissed me off! Because the only thing I hate more than extra
calories is not even remembering how they tasted. *PIP* is
hosted by a place called Magazzini Generali, which should be
avoided any other day of the week. I still don't understand
what part of town this place is in. Once I went to sleep in
someone's car in the parking lot because I didn't know how to
get home.

Sunday: PLASTIC

Plastic is Iconic! International superstars have danced on that
floor, kissed on those couches and vomited in those toilets!
They have parties all weekend but I go on Sundays because
Sundays are free. On Sundays they play French dance music

and old-school Italian stuff that makes you nostalgic for something you never had, like…success, glamour, a father figure, etc. There's a Chinese bar across the street from Plastic, where everyone goes before the club opens to drink cheap-as-dirt cocktails. The Chinese Bar is often the best part of the night because people relax there. Nobody relaxes at Plastic. I've tried to and when I did I was kicked out. Two times! I have a scar on my left eyelid from when a drag queen pushed me into a corner of the "mirror room." Apparently, I was dancing on her cube— an offense punishable by death. Everyone stared at me as I walked around. I thought, "damn, I'm on fire tonight!" Then I went to the bathroom and saw my face was covered in blood. I splashed vodka on it and kept dancing. My boyfriend says the scar suits me.

Monday: NOTHING

On Monday Satan rests! Not because I want to, just because there's nothing else to do. I should start a Monday night party. I'd call it: MERDA FRITTA. But I can't start my party while I work for someone else's.

Things used to be less complicated. I used to party alone. I'd get ready alone, take the tram alone, walk there alone, go inside alone, get my drinks alone, dance alone and go home alone, crying. It's tough getting "IN" with the Milanese Party Crowd when you don't dress well and can't speak Italian.

That's where sex comes in handy: it's a universal language. After a few months of screwing the right dealers and promoters I got myself stuck in a social spider web so sticky I almost miss the nights I got to sit by myself at a bar, pretending to text someone who was "late" to meet me. Now when I go out I have to juggle my boss, my friends and my boyfriend. Anyway, I'll figure them out after I get dressed.

Here's my "glamour" routine: I shower when I've got time

but when I don't I take an "Italian Shower" meaning I bidet my butt. I change my underwear and tights, moisturize and put on deodorant. I may change my dress or I may not. I change into a higher pair of heels. I own several pairs of shoes, all black heels, some nicer than others. (Ranging from *H&M* to *ZARA* to *Something My Mom Bought Me For Christmas*). I actually do like colors other than black—I'm punk, not Goth. But it just makes sense, financially, to invest in a color that goes unnoticed.

Nobody realizes when I wear the same dress three days in a row!... Right? I wash my morning makeup off and put on the exact same makeup on again: porcelain CoverGirl face powder, Mac black liquid eyeliner, "Russian Red" Mac lipstick, and tons of Lancôme mascara. Until spiders are crawling out of my eyes I'm not satisfied! I put some perfume on, either *Lola* by Marc Jacobs or *Poison* by Dior. I load on the hairspray. My jet-black bob should be a helmet, with a bit of blue shine that comes from grocery store boxed dye. And, voila! You know that comic book character, VALENTINA? I'm her androgynous cousin with a Slavic nose.

5. PUPA

"None of you would think I'm hot without all the makeup I wear on my vagina." I Tweet that with my Nokia. There's a phone number I can Tweet to directly. Like, you text this phone number as if it's a person, but it's not, it's Twitter. When you text Twitter your Tweet is posted on the Twitter website. Tweeting makes me look like I'm constantly texting a friend. I use most of my phone credit on it. I can't check the likes until I've got my laptop and WIFI. I usually only get a few likes because nobody uses Twitter except for funny celebrities, depressed students and horny robots. But it's cooler than Facebook. My boss and my boyfriend have Blackberries and I want one so bad. Can you imagine checking Twitter from anywhere?

Things I'd do for a Blackberry:

1. Spend a night in Stazione Centrale
2. Send my nudes to my parents
3. Ride bus 90 naked
4. Poop my pants in public

5. Eat 10,000 calories in one sitting
6. I'll probably end up doing all of these things and still not get a Blackberry.

Oh crap, my boyfriend's calling! I always call him first, when I leave the office. I've got a ten minute walk from there to NABA and we talk the whole time. NABA stands for "Nuova Accademia di Belli Arti" but I think it should stand for "Noi Amiamo Droga, Bukkake, Anale!" NABA is like Marangoni, if Marangoni were totally unknown. It's like IED, if IED had hippies instead of professors. It's like Accademia di Brera, if the iconic architecture of the Brera academy were replaced with a LIDL supermarket. You get the picture. The campus has got a cool bar, though. NABAR—smart name, right? You can't say they don't try. I've got classes from 17:30-21:30 every night. Lezioni serali, che stile. Tonight, I skipped class and don't want my boyfriend to know. Months into this relationship, seeing his name on my phone is a punch in the stomach. Ouch!

"Hey!" I sound too enthusiastic.

"Hey baby. Where are you?"

I open my fridge and pull out a box of Tavernello.

"In school."

"Don't lie to me."

"How's work going?"

"Boring. I wish you were under my desk."

"Are we meeting later?"

"I have a dinner, then I'm free."

I chug some Tavernello. Who the hell is he having dinner with? Why not me? Oh, right, I don't eat dinner. "Cool! I'm free until midnight, then I have a party—"

"Have fun." He hangs up.

"Goddamnit!" I throw my phone on the sofa.

"Ouch!" Maria yells. I didn't see her.

"Sorry, Maria."

. . .

My boyfriend hates my friends. He thinks it's sad that we hang out until sunrise doing drugs. I think it's sad that he doesn't. My people aren't bad. It took me a long time to find them and even longer to make them like me. When I first got here my best friend was Skype. My boys back in Boone were always awake doing something reckless. And they were always in need of an audience. The six hour difference made no difference.

"Look, it's your favorite." Jack looked thinner and sicker and hotter each time we Skyped. He held a blue balloon filled with magic up to the camera.

"Black tar? Jealous! Ok, I need to get dressed."

"You look great in that." He heated up a spoon.

"Jack, I'm in underwear. And I'm going to be late!"

"Just stay with me while I do this. Please."

"Of course, sorry." I can't believe I was so rude. I may have been late for work but it's bad manners to let someone get smashed alone.

"So, the Mexicans say hi." He got out a cotton ball.

"Y'all drove there *again*? Who pays for the gas?"

"Coby's parents." He sucked the liquid into the syringe. It looked clean, that's a relief. It used to be my job to get new ones. Boys get lazy about that stuff, as they do with everything.

"How's Coby doing?" Coby is my ex-boyfriend. I cheated on Coby with Jack.

Then I cheated on them both with George. Nobody got mad. By then their junk barely worked anymore. I simply needed all three of them to make one reliable boyfriend.

"He's not doing good." He wrapped his arm in a latex band. That impressed me, because he used to use shoelaces. "We aren't doing good."

"Yeah, me neither." I couldn't find any clean tights.

"Shut up." He flicked the syringe.

"I'm serious."

"You're in MILAN!" He shot up. "Have…" His head fell on his shoulder, like someone asleep on a bus.

"…have what?"

"…fun."

I only do "party drugs" now. Cocaine cut with baby laxatives, bitter MDMA crystals sprinkled into vodka Redbull, Ketamine that makes me feel like an alien fetus dancing in Cicciolina's womb. Random pills found in pockets. Boys, here's a tip: when girls say, "I'm freezing, can I wear your jacket?" They aren't really cold. You should know this— weather can't touch party girls. The truth is they want your coat on their backs because they hope to steal your high. Jackpot! Then they only blow you to make sure the blue pills they got from your wallet aren't Viagra.

Most nights go like this for me:

I go out and have a dozen drinks.

Someone gives me something and I take it.

I forget about it and have a dozen drinks.

I say, "I don't feel good. I think someone drugged me!"

I think about my mom randomly and feel guilty.

I say, "someone take me home I need to sleep!"

I remember that I'm a legend who doesn't sleep.

I say, "where is the after-party?"

I realize I'm talking to a cockroach on the street and it's noon.

Magro and Frank have good stuff. They give it to me for free. Now that I think about it, I haven't paid for any drugs since I got my new job. Being used isn't a bad thing. It literally means that you're useful. I think they even flirt with me sometimes. I think that if I lost ten kilos, grew out my hair, changed my wardrobe and my personality and my habits and my tastes and everything I think and care about, and, like, my DNA, I may have a chance with them. But probably not.

The only issue I have with my friends is they don't do anything. When I got here I thought that people my age would have jobs. Or hobbies, at least. In America you have to "do" stuff. It's cool to be productive. Poor kids flip burgers, middle class kids do internships and rich kids volunteer. The extra-cool kids also play in bands and rob houses.

Here, my peers like to show off how they waste their lives away. I guess it's because Europeans have "history" and "lineage" and "culture" and it's nice to show everyone around you that the people you came from set you up for life, with a family home and a family discount at Esselunga. I don't know. That's just my theory. Anyway, all my friends do is shop, party and go to restaurants. Good for them! I'm not jealous or whatever. I swear. It just sucks that when I want to sleep for a few hours, because I have responsibilities, they don't understand. My friends have filled their brains to the brim with mood boards of Margiela. There's no room left for empathy.

They can't help but sabotage me.

I open one eye and see exposed brick. I open the other and see Flow. She blows smoke in my face and I inhale it. Flow is a loud girl with a gap-toothed grin. She's from the Dominican Republic. Her past is a mystery. So is how she pays rent. She has a street level loft on the Naviglio. It's the second best after-party spot. The best after-party spot is Via Malaga, a dozen lofts facing each other in a gated block. Most people leave their doors wide open and hop back and forth between places. Only models, dealers and DJs live there. Via Malaga is also known as The Road to Hell. Why the hell am I here again?

"Come on! Be a rock star!" Flow pleads. Music is blasting and people are dancing and sitting around on the sofa. I fell asleep in her bed in the same room.

"I have to work in two hours!" The mailing lists flash before my eyes. I should have studied in high school. I could have been a veterinarian.

"So take another line!" Flow cuts some speed on a mirror. Her lines are always straight and even. So talented.

"Ok, make it big."

I embrace peer pressure. It's led me to where I am, as a person. Since puberty, peer pressure has been my guiding light, in the place of God. So I stay up and do more lines. Shower in her bathroom. Change into the undies I've got in my purse. Check her medicine cabinets for pills, perfume and moisturizer. And when I leave for the office, they all go to sleep. Losers!

My boyfriend doesn't take my calls when I'm with my friends or when I'm leaving an after-party. And that's a problem because I'm spending more and more time doing both. Only ONCE did I call him ten times in a row at ten in the morning in a crazed comedown...and now he won't let me forget it. Whatever, he's just jealous. He wishes I were with him instead. I used to sleep over at his place every night and soon any night will become impossible.

We've only got a few months left, of life as we know it. It's November now and *she* comes back in January. I never thought I could hate someone so much without knowing them. Not in the way you hate an evil politician like Anna Wintour or a stupid reality star like Berlusconi. This is personal, I feel attacked. My friends were like, "how can you bang a married man?" and, "what about the wife?"

I was like, "what about the wife? She's *also* banging a married man!"

They didn't get it.

I asked him what we're going to do when she moves back

in with him. He said, "I don't want to think about it." I think it's a good sign.

He thinks his friends are more "sophisticated" than mine but they aren't.

They're just older. They're in their forties and fifties. Artists, photographers, scammers, creeps, whatever. Dudes who like Woody Allen. Men who seem interesting only when they talk about stuff they did back when I was a baby. His closest friend used to take all the photos of Pete Doherty, like every picture of Pete that isn't taken by the paparazzi. Now he takes naked pictures of me.

What a downgrade!

My boyfriend and his friends call themselves "La Banda" and they call me "La Pupa Della Banda." I have no idea what that means and I'm not going to ask. They probably only call me that because they don't remember my name. I'm not sure if my boyfriend even likes them. He seems annoyed most of the time. Sometimes he leaves them-all of us-randomly. Once we were all driving somewhere in a car and when we stopped at a light, he opened the door and got out. We were like, "Dude, che cazzo fai?" and he just ran away. I think he only hangs out with them because he's in control. I guess he only hangs out with me for the same reason.

I am good at pleasing tyrants.

Here's the secret: control freaks, sociopaths, psychos, sadists, boyfriends and bosses don't realize that what they do to me is a piece of cake compared to what I've done to myself. Yet the sacrifice seems so impressive. My ability to throw myself in the trash for their sake makes me delightful in relationships and excellent at my job!

But joke's on them. I love the trash.

I admired my boss for months before she hired me. I'd always see her around town with a hot young boy on her arm, a fancy dress on her body, a blonde wig on her head. A devilish look in her eyes. She is *so* London. A mix of *Absolutely Fabulous* and Rimmel ads. "Get the London look! Or else!"

My boss is in her late thirties but she's got the body of a teenager. Her face is sharp and soft in all the right places and only looks "her age" because she's always pissed off. Everyone is either too slow, too dumb, too ugly or too Italian for her. She's suspicious, paranoid and incredibly harsh but she is adored by everyone, including me.

"You're a blessing, Mia."

She lights herself a cigarette and hands me one.

"This cigarette is a blessing!"

Compliments are embarrassing but my responses to compliments are disturbing. I should kill myself.

"I had to fire everyone."

"Really?" I act surprised but I've been told the stories. The warnings.

"Before you came I was alone."

I know. "Wow."

"I was so betrayed."

That's not what I heard. "That sucks."

"You can't trust anyone."

Including you? "OK."

"I'm done." She flicks her cigarette and steps on it, after just a few puffs.

"I'm almost done."

"Mia! Put it out!"

"Oh! Yes, sorry." I stomp it out and look up. She's already gone.

Her office is a little room on the second floor of some other office. She decorated the space with framed flyers from her parties. She's got coffee table books that each weigh more than she does, stacked against the walls. Hundreds of them. The kinds of books you buy at 10 Corso Como or Dover

Street Market and never open. But she opens hers all the time. She's a walking collection of references.

What I have in common with her is this basic ideal: while some people think a last name, bank account or set of tits define you, her and I think a person is defined by which bands and movies they like. What I don't have in common with her is that, in addition to her impressive pop culture savvy, she also has a good last name, a fat bank account and the perfect set of tits.

Working for her has changed my life overnight. I feel like that Jenny character in *Gossip Girl* when she finally starts hanging out with Blair. Of course Blair is a bitch but she's a fabulous one. My boyfriend makes fun of me whenever I talk about my boss. Big surprise, he doesn't like her. When he takes me out and his intellectual blah blah acquaintances ask what I do, I say I work for Her, and my boyfriend laughs, and says, "Baby, nobody knows who that is."

Yeah? Maybe your grandpa friends don't know the hottest publicist town, but anyone who matters does. I do! My boss doesn't like him, either. They're so resentful about each other sometimes I wonder if they're hiding something.

"How old is your boyfriend, anyway?" My boss talks fast between bites of arugula. We have lunch at our desk and during that time we always gossip. Every day at 13:00 I go out and pick up two salads with tomato and mozzarella. Two bottles of sparkling water. She says she used to have eating issues, like me, and that the trick to a good body is actually eating three meals a day. Hah! Nonsense. She was bulimic, that's an eating disorder with a budget.

"Um...I think he's your age?"

"Excuse me?"

"I mean, he's definitely older, never mind."

"Well, I don't get what you're doing with him."

"Yeah, I used to date models and stuff."

"I don't mean that, I'm not superficial. I also like them rough."

"Well what do you mean?"

"I think he's using you."

"For what? I'm useless!" I laugh.

She doesn't.

"Just be careful, I've got a bad feeling about him."

I skip school again tonight because my boss is taking me to some cocktail parties. Once I told her that I shouldn't miss so much school for work and she told me to "grow up." Once she suggested I quit school and become "serious" about Public Relations.

I've practically quit school already. But if I really did it my boyfriend would kill me. He's obsessed with school because he's a professor at Bocconi. I bet he seduces all of his students. Once, when we were laying in bed at his place, he told me that he wishes he could buy me an apartment, next door to his. He said he would make it out of glass so he could always watch me. He said he would lock me in a cage and make me study all day. I said that sounds like torture because I hate to study.

Tomorrow night will work out better. La Banda is hosting a party at PRAVDA for the release of their porn magazine. The one I'm in. I've finally made it, mom! I haven't told my boss yet about this commitment but I'm sure she'll let me go.

"Last call for cocktails!" My boss is in her element. She's surrounded by gays and a few kiss-ass boys she'll take to bed. She doesn't need me anymore.

"I think I'm going home."

"Mia, here-for the month." She gives me 500 euros cash. She always hands me my "under the table" payment under an actual table.

My boyfriend says I deserve to get paid more, since I'm always on call, like a doctor. What is he talking about? I'm basically rich now. At this rate I may be able to move out of my place…maybe I could even get my own room, with a door!

I leave the Grand Hotel et de Milan and walk down the street to smoke a cigarette. Milan is pretty cute at night. Whenever I get paid I treat myself to a taxi.

But first, more importantly, before I forget: *"Whoever said life isn't a popularity contest clearly wasn't alive."* Tweet sent.

Now I'm out of phone credit. Cazzo! How will I call my car?

6. GENTLEMEN'S CLUB

Like most couples, we met at a porn shoot. Ok, that's a lie. We met at an art gallery but we hooked up at a porn shoot. The art gallery was somewhere hideous, like Piola. I try to avoid art events at all costs but my friend Cat made me come. She's also from the Dominican Republic. She knows Flow from there. Cat is an enigma. She says she's an actress but all I see her acting is in love with her ugly boyfriend.

She has an apartment in the center, right by San Babila station. It's insane.

So she took me to this art thing with her dumb boyfriend who is friends with, you guessed it: my boyfriend.

I was dressed extra badly that night. I was wearing something I made for NABA. I hate sewing more than I hate studying. But they force me to do my own sewing to create my designs. Which makes no sense, and is totally unfair, since the architecture students don't have to build their own buildings! The design students don't have to craft their own chairs! The graphic students don't have to construct their own....computers! Ok, metaphor stretched a bit, but you get it. Fashion design professors are oppressors. I tried to make this Vivienne Westwood looking skirt but it ended up looking like a restaurant napkin looks after you wipe your butt with it because you ran out of toilet paper. And now the toilet is clogged and you are wearing an ugly skirt to an art gallery where you're about to meet the person you're going to be in love with. I was also wearing American Apparel leggings, an American Apparel leotard, an H&M coat, and some platform shoes I was holding together with tape.

Cat said to me, "My boyfriend's friends need a model for their new project. Are you interested?"

"Do they need a hand model? Because I don't know if you see who you're talking to."

"Haha! No, it's not fashion modeling. It's nude. Very artistic."

"OK. I've always wanted to be a nude hand model," I said.

She lead me to a group of the ugliest guys I've ever seen. I leaned into her neck and whispered, "You've got to be kidding me!"

There were five or six of them, standing around like a bunch of perverts caught jerking off in a park, waiting to be taken to jail. One guy stood out the most, though. He was the tallest, he was bald and he had really piercing eyes, like they had lasers in them. He made me feel uncomfortable. When he looked at me I wanted to hide in the bathroom. Yeah, that's him.

"We're making this artistic erotica magazine," the white-haired guy said.

"We need a centerfold," the fat guy said.

"You'd be perfect for it," my future boyfriend said.

"Sure." Why not? I hate my body so much I may as well let it get objectified.

I gave them my number and went outside for a smoke. I spotted a pigeon and considered it a sign that I made the right choice. Then I spotted another pigeon and figured there's no such thing.

A photographer I never met picked me up a week later. He was doughy, with unwashed clothes and a wiry moustache. He drove me an hour out of town. Somewhere pointless, like Monza. I tried to make small talk on the way but he didn't seem to speak English or understand my Italian. We parked at an abandoned villa.

"Is this your place?" I asked.

"No."

"It's right out of a Tim Burton movie."

No response. He must be more of a Tarantino guy. The place was big and spooky. Spiderwebs and white sheets hung onto everything. This must be the local crack house for kids with an inheritance. I checked the floors for needles.

"Where's the bathroom?"

"I don't know. Don't use it."

We started in a Victorian bedroom. I pictured a princess poisoning herself.

"Take your clothes off." He pointed to the bed and tinkered with his camera. I left a black pile on the floor and hopped onto the filthy fabric. "Any bug can be a bed bug if you love it hard enough." *I've gotta remember to Tweet that.*

I propped myself on my side and he put a ribbon over my eyes and tied it up from behind. I laid in different positions and heard clicks. He led me through the house. I laid on dusty carpets, broken furniture and at one point, a mirror. The shoot was uneventful. Then again, I couldn't see anything. Maybe I got gang-banged by ghosts.

My future boyfriend got the pictures developed and emailed them to me.

"I like the one where I'm on my stomach." I wrote. "It's kind of chic."

"Baby, this isn't a fashion magazine," he replied.

He was unimpressed. He wanted a re-shoot, and he

wanted to be involved. When I emailed him back asking what he had in mind, he called me. His voice made me feel so dirty I had to step outside to talk. I didn't want Maria to hear me dealing with the devil. He told me to meet him and his friends at a bar that weekend.

That night I was hosting a party for my boss at the Triennale museum, so I was dressed up pretty well. I had on these strappy sandals I could hardly walk in and a black polyester dress that always got stuck between my butt cheeks. I had to run to my meeting with the guys so I was sweaty by the time I arrived.

My future boyfriend sat close to me as we discussed the shoot. His friends said they saw "raw potential" in my pictures and they didn't want to waste all that on a photographer who was "uninspired." They wanted to do something special, geared towards my tastes, something involving a "male talent." The guy who shot Pete Doherty's biography would be shooting me. I told him I'm a huge fan of Daddy Doherty and I'll do anything (anything!) as long as he sends Pete the photos.

"For location we're thinking...seedy, grimy, nasty," the photographer said.

"Sounds like my apartment," I replied.

"You OK posing with one of our friends?"

"As long as he isn't an ex."

I felt my future boyfriend's leg push into mine. I didn't move.

"Would you like to write Pete a letter?"

"What kind of letter?"

"To go with your editorial. A full page of your feelings for Pete."

"Hell yeah!" What if Pete falls in love with me and we get married and —

My future boyfriend put his hand on my knee, looked in my eyes and said, "Your shoes drive me crazy."

"Try walking in them!" I yelped.

He laughed. I usually am won over by anyone who laughs at my jokes but the way he did it made me uneasy. I made a mental note to myself to not get closer to him.

I guess the note got lost in the mail.

7. FIGA D'ORO

La Banda picked me up on a muggy summer night. The air was damp and heavy. Even the mosquitos were annoyed. I had to sit on their laps in the back of a car. Something small and basic, like a Fiat or Ferrari or...Fendi? I don't know. My dad is a mechanic but I couldn't recognize a car if it hit me!

When I used to get driven to school every day by this boy, Sam, he would first take me out for coffee. And every morning, after coffee, I would stand next to the wrong car. Not his. He thought I did it to be funny.

I wore a transparent black mesh American Apparel dress with nothing underneath. I had a black polyester H&M robe on over it. I was soaked in sweat in minutes. My hands and feet are always sweaty but the combination of anxiety, summer in Milan, synthetic fabric and sitting on the laps of horny men made it worse. Even my butthole was sweaty. Oh, I also wore those strappy sandals that drove my future boyfriend "crazy."

We stopped at an AutoGrill to pick up beers. Everyone was in high spirits. We each drank a warm pint at the bar and packed the rest into the trunk of the car. They'd bought a carton.

"Why do we need so much beer?" I asked.

"In case your pussy gets thirsty."

I hate when men use that word. My future boyfriend was in the front seat before. Now he sat in the back so I could sit on him. He hugged my thighs tightly and I felt him get hard.

"I like you. You're old fashioned," he said into my hair.

"What do you mean? I'm 70's punk or 90's riot grrrl?"

After half an hour or so we stopped in a parking lot and parked the car. We all got out, stretched and looked around. Middle of nowhere, abandoned, dirty. Sublime!

Another car pulled up. A short, scraggly, hairy little runt man got out. He stank, in every way. He was introduced to me as the "male talent." Wait. WHAT? I took my future boyfriend aside and asked what the hell they were thinking.

"What the hell were you thinking?"

"He's not cute but he has a huge dick," he assured me.

"Do I look like I care about that?"

"Just relax and have fun."

Great advice, jerk.

I got back into the car and started posing. The photographer took some pictures. The gross guy got into the car and tried to kiss me and I pushed him away. I got out of the car. I found another place to pose. The boys took the beer out of the trunk and started pouring it all over me. Close up shots of beer pouring into my mouth, on my chest, on my stomach... Then the gross guy came back. My mood dropped.

My future boyfriend channeled his inner Disney prince and pushed him out of the way. Then he picked me up and held me in his arms. He actually carried me away from the shoot! (Being carried made me feel super skinny, I recommend it.) After a few minutes he set me on top of a radiator behind a building. There, he kissed me. Then, he pushed my dress up and fingered me for the first time.

"Mia. Hai una figa d'oro."

After I faked an orgasm, he said we should get back to the

shoot. He walked me to an empty garage. He took my dress off over my head and tied my arms behind my back with it. He pushed me down to my knees and slapped me in the face. Then he went down on me, on camera.

It was exhilarating to watch, outside of my body.

I didn't come back into my body until a day or so afterwards.

8. SWINGERS

My boss is stressed today because her maid shrunk her Prada sweater in the washing machine. This morning she asked me to come over with coffee because she was running late to the office. I didn't know why until I heard her screaming. "Do you not read the labels?! I guess it's my daughter's sweater now!!" I felt bad for the maid but then I remembered that she gets paid more than me and has regular, set hours and doesn't have to do coke with her. And then I felt bad for myself.

"Hey it's 17:00, I've gotta run to school."

"You can't go."

"I can do the mailing list from class!"

"No school tonight, I need you." She has that mean crease between her eyebrows. She only allows herself to wrinkle her forehead on special occasions. I'm doomed.

"For what?"

"I have a dinner party at my house with Frank and Magro."

"Oh. Well that sounds fun but I have a party I can't miss."

"I didn't ask you. This is work."

"How is it work?"

"I need your help!"

"And usually I'd love to help! But tonight is important! The whole party is for me, basically."

"Is it your birthday?"

"No, it's the launch party of a magazine. I'm the centerfold!"

"Do they employ you? Do they pay you?"

"No, but—"

"Finish the mailing list. Then we'll get ready. You'll have fun. I know you have a crush on Frank!"

"I have a crush on both of them, actually."

"Ok! So, you should thank me! Magazines are dead, anyway."

"Not porn magazines."

"What?"

"Nothing."

My boss's apartment looks the way a teen girl hopes her adult apartment will look like: Cher's home in *Clueless*, the tour bus in *Spice World* and a Miu Miu boutique. The sun shines brighter in here. Every surface is sparkling and femme. Her bed is covered in marshmallow fluff. The air smells like candy. Her carpets are bouncier than a new pair of Nikes (not that I've ever worn sneakers). Boxes of Prada stilettos, Gucci sandals, Fendi boots and Dolce & Gabbana pumps stacked against the bedroom wall form a pyramid so grand, it must have been built by slaves. Or aliens. Or enslaved aliens. Racks of clothes that don't fit into the walk-in closet hang out in hallways. Couture pieces and accessories borrowed from designers for some event, then forgotten about, have become relics. They come alive at night and socialize.

Her kitchen looks like a film set of a kitchen, because it practically is. There are just enough ingredients around to feel "provided for" but not triggered. I wouldn't be surprised if most of it was prop food stolen from furniture stores. Glass fruits and plastic pastries. Her fridge is lined with turquoise bottles of sparkling water. The freezer has only special edition vodka, tequila and gin. Did you know Cavalli makes alcohol? Wild. All this and no husband in sight. A dream come true.

She's really good at making salads. She's made a few for me. Every leaf tastes like something other than a leaf but I can't figure out why. I cover all the food I eat in ketchup or Tabasco sauce to hide the fact that I'm always eating something tasteless. This isn't her method. She has a delicate touch. She cares. Nothing is excessively oily or salty or spicy...it just is. In another life, she was a gardener or a shaman.

In another life, I am more like her.

She keeps other, non-salad foods around just for her guests. I don't count as a guest. Most of her guests are coke-heads or fit gay men (or both) so none of them ever require more than a handful of nuts or a non-sweaty cheese cube, three olives from a martini, Asian bar snacks made from seaweed. Nothing that could produce crumbs, stains or odors. Her home is a safe-haven for her emotional and physical well-being. It's as tended to as her mailing lists. No signs of anything related to self-harm, destructive behaviors or laziness. Crazy!

But not even my boss has control over the outside world and she is a professional socializer, after all. She surrenders herself to consumption-heavy Italian affairs. I have witnessed her eating a plate of milky mozzarella, a bowl of dense cacio peppe and a creamy tiramisu at a work dinner once. She didn't disappear into the bathroom or get visibly depressed. She just ate, drank and laughed.

In her Real Life, I'm guessing she only eats her wonderful salads, which explains how she can have "three meals a day" and stay tiny. She reminds me of Kylie Minogue. I wonder if Kylie Minogue is a bitch. Small, pointy women are usually bitches, they must be, otherwise people will step on them, literally. I'm tall and big-boned so I have bad posture, a habit large girls pick up, trying to make themselves as small as their friends. I'll become one of those old ladies so bent over they can only look at the ground. I'll be a letter "C." I'll hold myself up with a shopping cart full of bread crumbs and seeds for my birds.

In her movie set kitchen she moves with purpose and grace, like a TV mom.

"Dinner's done, get ready!" She holds up a bag of spinach.

The guests are on their way so I head to her glorious bathroom. I touch up my makeup, use her bidet and douse myself in perfumes. She's got a dozen bottles of the good designer stuff. I like making obscene combinations, like Chanel *no.5* with Mugler's *Alien*. My wrists are a lady but my neck is a skank. A sell-out in the streets but street-cred in the sheets! After a few minutes I smell like a department store and my butthole is so clean you could drink prosecco out of it. I need to stop procrastinating. I send my boyfriend the text I've been dreading all evening.

"My boss won't let me leave."

"How late are you?"

"I'm not late. I'm not coming."

"You're kidding."

"I'm sorry."

A minute passes. No answer.

I put more perfume on. No answer.

Is he trying to kill me??? I text him again.

"I'm SO sorry."

"Sorry is useless. Be angry."

"I am!"

"Does she know that you are angry?"

"It wouldn't matter."

"You let her push you around."

At least she pays me to obey her; what's his excuse?

"How's the big launch?"

"Pointless without our star."

Don't cry, dumb bitch. Give yourself something to look forward to.

"Let's meet tomorrow?"

"She's here tomorrow."

I look down and let tears drop. A model taught me the trick. If you tilt your head down and open your eyes wide as you cry the tears plop right out without smearing your mascara. I focus on the bathroom tiles to calm my nerves. Drop drop drop.

"MIA! What are you doing in there?"

"Oh! Sorry, I had to poop!"

"Ew! Keep that to yourself! The boys are here, come out!"

You know that Rancid song that goes: *"Black coat, white shoes, black hat, Cadillac, yeah! The boy's a time bomb!"* I always think of it when I see them. They look like they get dressed together. They look like they're in a band that wears uniforms, like The Hives. They look like the boys from *A Clockwork Orange*, with all the colors inversed. Being close to them or being looked at by them or having a conversation with them always makes me want to throw myself off of the roof of the LaRinascente. I wonder what horrible things they say about me when I'm gone. How they must laugh! It's just my boss, Frank, Magro and me tonight. This will be torture.

Before I can start calculating the calories I had in spinach, our plates are taken away. A new plate arrives, but it's not for dessert. The porcelain has been heated slightly to enhance the performance of our party powder. The hyenas pounce.

"Who goes first?" Magro asks, going first.

"I'll have the smallest," my boss insist, snagging the largest.

"Che merda," Frank spits, doing two in a row.

I push the remains into a sloppy line and lick the plate.

Milanese coke is crap. It's cut with speed, maybe meth, probably opiates but not the fun ones. Everyone complains about the baby laxatives mixed in. Those don't affect me. At "rock bottom" I've taken twenty laxative pills at once. When I was "recovering" senior year and started eating again I couldn't stand it. When I felt the food sitting in my stomach I wanted to rip it out. And I can't make myself vomit. So in a panic I'd leave home or school or piano lessons or whatever and walk to the nearest supermarket-often miles away-and steal a pack of poop pills. I'd take all of the pills at once, in the bathroom of the grocery store, then walk back to wherever I was and crap my brains out. Sometimes I'd be on the toilet all night and all day. It was pure agony, but better than having a small meal digesting properly inside of me.

I thought anal was so painful for me because of my past habits. But after talking to every other girl on the planet about it I've confirmed that it's just anal. It's evil. I don't understand why men hate us so much to put us through it. I think when men want to do anal they should do it with other men, who have those prostate things.

My favorite sex positions:

1. Missionary. This is actually the only position in which I get any friction on my clit so it's the only position in which I may ever have a chance at having an orgasm. Also it's comfortable because I can play dead.
2. Doggy style. This is basically like the "cat-cow" yoga stuff which is really good for your posture. If the TV is on and I can watch it that's a plus.
3. That's it, everything else is exhausting.

I wonder if Frank and Magro have ever done each other in the butt. I wonder what their dicks are like. Men's dicks are always a mirror of the man they're attached to. Girls get disappointed because they don't ask the right questions. They say, "if he's tall it's big if his fingers are short it's small." So wrong. What about the spirit of the dick? The character of it? How would the dick dress if he wore clothes? I bet that Frank and Magro's dicks write poetry in café's all day while smoking Lucky Strikes.

I'm bored and I want to go home but not to my home.

It took three dates to see my boyfriend's dick. Our relationship really is old-fashioned. Our first date, he took me to a strip club. We got a private room with a stripper and both made out with her. I didn't realize how expensive private dances are and I made him pay for several sessions which emptied him out for the night. After, he took me to his place but we were wasted so we just made out. The next morning he told me that I "look perfect" in the vintage bathing suit that I wear as underwear. Then he made me tea and I went to work. Then I thought about what he said all day.

The next night he took me to an escort bar. I didn't know these places existed. You have to know where they are or get invited to them, or something. I guess men are on mailing lists for those kinds of things. It's basically a bar full of tables with an escort or two sitting at each. If you sit down with them you are expected to buy them a drink. If you hit it off, you take them home. In that way, it's like any other bar people go to. The women looked beautiful and bored. I met this Croatian lady who was nice to me. She said she could see me working there! I was flattered. She also said that she generally liked her job but that she hated men like the ones I came in with, who waste her time. I forgot to mention the whole Banda tagged along on this date. They were rude to the women and bought zero drinks. I apologized for their sake and bought her and her colleagues some cocktails. Then I went home because I felt bad about spending a week's worth of money.

When he told me he was taking me to a Swinger's Club I lost it. Our third date would be the most glamorous night of my life! It would be a mix of Studio 54 and Andy Warhol's Factory and Richard Hell's living room and Cicciolina's daydreams, directed by Steven Klein. I put a mood board together in my head on the way there in his car. The color palette would be *Blue Velvet* by David Lynch. The women there would be Siouxie Sioux, Nina Hagen and Brigitte Nielsen. The men would be all of the Ramones, Tony Hawk, and my boyfriend. I was going to die, absolutely DROP DEAD the second I stepped foot in the place!

And then...I stepped foot in that place.

Is this...a joke?

Because it's not funny.

There is no guest list. No art direction. Nobody I'd like to screw!

They let anyone in here! Anyone who is willing to pay. Obviously I didn't have to, but I imagine that it costs a ton, because the men inside looked so thirsty to get their money's worth. I don't recall seeing any attractive couples, or any women, actually. Just lots of sfigati looking for a figa.

My boyfriend took me to a room. It wasn't really a "room" because there was no door, just curtains. Everything was dark brown. The carpet, the wallpaper and the bed. He laid me down, lifted my dress up and started to screw me. As far as dicks go I admit his is outstanding. Just as I started enjoying myself some dumbasses opened our curtains.

A couple dudes in fleece jackets and sweatpants took their junk out and started jerking off. I didn't say anything but I did look away. My boyfriend said do you like being watched? And I said not by those guys and he told them to leave and they did.

I guess it was the nicest thing a guy ever did.

Afterwards we had a drink at the bar and he accused me of faking it. I did, obviously, but I couldn't tell him that. He didn't know that I faked with everyone! He would have taken it personally! Sex with him was fine, as far as sex with another person goes. He said, "I fucked you like I'd fuck my mother. Next time will be different." Yeah, next time we need door selection for who can enter our VIP room.

"*Vaginas are the original VIP rooms,*" I Tweeted.

"What are you doing?" he peered over my phone.

"What?" I put my phone face-down on the bar.

"Who are you texting?"

"Twitter," I said.

"Who?"

"Oh, just one of the guys who was watching us."

9. FAKE FUR

When it comes to masturbation, I was a prodigy. I had my first orgasm at six. I became addicted, as I do with everything. Addiction addict. I masturbated whenever I could. Every night before bed, each time I took a bath, on the sofa when cartoons got boring, in the kitchen while waiting for popcorn to microwave. I had messed up fantasies, too. About my teachers, my neighbors and the pizza delivery guy. I had a recurring storyline about my gym teacher keeping me in a storage closet.

Great dialogue, too. I could write porno scripts.

I still wasn't sure how sex worked but I had a general idea, based on how my older sister and her friends played with their Barbies. I remember I had this amazing outfit in that storyline, a transparent plastic two-set skirt with a top that pressed down on my baby boobies. A designer in the making, for sure. My girlfriends growing up didn't jerk off, or at least they didn't admit to it. But once they got boyfriends in high school, they had orgasms with them. Or at least they said they did.

Sometimes I'm grateful for my 'finishing' problem. If I could splooge during sex, I'd be a monster. I'd probably be in prison. I can't believe that men get to cum every time they do it. Unless they're drunk or worried about soccer. No wonder they're such shitheads. The world really isn't fair for women. Or at least it's unfair to me.

If I've met you I've probably jerked off to you. Don't be flattered, it doesn't mean I like you. The less I like you the more likely I am to jerk off to you. When I'm dating a guy I never can jerk off to him. I have to think about one of his friends or the bartender who served us drinks or the homeless guy we passed while walking home. Otherwise I can't get off. If I've already had sex with you it means I don't get off thinking about you. That's the difference between other boys and my boyfriend. I save the images of what we do in bed, replay them in my head and cum like a queen! I wonder if he does the same. He told me once, when we first started doing it, that he replayed "the scene" in his head the next day and that I reminded him of some movie, but I had never heard of the movie he mentioned, so he got annoyed, and then he never said anything like that again.

If God were real and I could ask her one question, it would be:

"Who has jerked off to me?"

If I could ask a second question it would be:

"Do the pigeons love me or just use me for bread?"

"Every time you have sex you have a threesome with God." I am so funny, wow.

"Mia, don't text in class."

"I'm not texting."

God, my professors are dumb. They don't know anything. Why am I supposed to listen to someone who can't even get into the parties I go to? As I see it, the whole point of going to fashion school is so that you make the right connections to get into fashion parties, where you can make the right connections to get fashion jobs. Well, I've already done all of that, and I was able to do that only because I skip school. I feel bad for my peers, they're clueless. They're tools. They study and sew their asses off for nothing. They're wasting their youth. I told my boyfriend that and he lectured me.

He was like, "Ten years from now you will be inviting your schoolmates to your silly parties. And they will be working for Bottega Veneta."

"First of all, I would *never* invite them to my parties. Secondly, who the fuck is Bottega Veneta?"

Everyone thinks that if they do their homework Donatella will kick down their door and beg them to design shoes for her. Bitch, please! This isn't Central Saint Martins. Vogue editors don't attend our fashion shows. We don't even have a fashion show! And even if we did, who cares? Hard work for the sake of hard work hasn't worked for anybody. If it did, my parents would be millionaires.

"I'm going to the bathroom!"

"Mia! Don't you dare!"

I sneak out like a raccoon slipping out of your garbage. I speed-walk and blast the Misfits so I can't hear her yelling. "Helena" is a brilliant song but it's so messed up. I listened to it for years without really hearing the lyrics. When I did, I felt sick, like when I peeled the breading off the frozen popcorn shrimp my dad made me when my mom worked late. I screamed, "THIS IS WHAT I WAS EATING?" and became vegetarian. Damn, did the professor really follow me outside? Povera puttana. Get a life!

I used to be a good student. As a kid you think that following rules and respecting authority figures will help you have a better life or something. Then you get your period and understand that everything is doomed and that you may as well avoid spending any minute of your life being told what to do.

I skipped class religiously in high school. After those Columbine shootings every public school got a cop. They'd walk around in full pig uniform, waving their big sticks around, intimidating us. The cops scared the kids more than they were ever scared of school shootings. Our campus cop was cool. With me, at least. Rex was my accomplice. I was his degenerate daughter. I bribed him with candy. Rex was taller than a Christmas Tree. He had a shaved head, scars on his face and a gun hanging off his belt. He looked vicious as a pitbull but was sweeter than the tootsie pops I'd slip in his pockets.

His smile brightened the halls when he'd see me. He'd pull on my pigtails and say, "you look like an anime character." I'd squeal, "you don't watch anime, loser!" Everyone thought we were dating. I was like, "I wish!" I knew by then that I was supposed to hate cops, but I figured, if I'm corrupting an officer to get what I want, that's actually extremely punk….right? Anyway, everyone was just jealous. He'd look the other way as I'd run across the lawn, then the football field, then the parking lot, and leave campus. Then, I was free. I could do whatever I wanted. With my legs, my Walkman and five dollars.

I couldn't do much. I'd walk around town. Check my reflection in dressing room mirrors of department stores. Shoplift some underwear. Hit up a Starbucks and write desperate stories in my journal while nursing an enormous black coffee. I'd stop by the Post Office, where the punks sat around. "Those punks sure have lots of letters to send!" The townies would joke, because they were stupid and didn't know anything.

Under the Post Office there was a basement. In the basement was a place called "Street Scene." It started out as a community center for poor kids. The poor kids all turned out to be punk rockers. The town hall paid for instruments, so the underprivileged youth could have a "wholesome" hobby. Those squares didn't realize that our type of music paired superbly with our other hobbies, which were sex and drugs.

We had a two electric guitars, one bass, one drum kit, a

couple amps and three microphones. Our little punk scene had a few decent bands. "Ass Piss," "Shit for Brains" and "The Rabid Possums." The elder punks got to use the equipment whenever they wanted and the younger punks got to use it when the elder punks were too wasted to move. The boys didn't want girls in their bands, so the girls had to be groupies. We'd sit around drinking 40oz malt liquor that homeless guys bought us for extra bucks, waiting for the boys to stop playing and start paying attention to us. There was a little stage the bands could play on, a dance floor and a bunch of couches stained with who knows what. Everyone got their first piercings down there, their first stick-n-poke tattoos, their first blowjobs. I met my first boyfriends in that basement. Boys from the other schools who also skipped class. Boys who weren't in school anymore. Who were never in school to begin with. They were free as flies. Their parents didn't care about them. So lucky!

To know you're leaving just as the party is getting started is a feeling that haunted me throughout my adolescence. Now I always stay out until everyone's gone to make up for lost time. I had to catch the bus home before my parents finished work. My whole life depended on our answering machine: DELETE DELETE DELETE!!!

The principal would call every day and say, "today Mia missed ___ classes" and "this is her ___ absence of the year." Then a secretary would call and repeat his message. Sometimes, the teachers called. "She's got potential, it's a shame to waste." Ma'am, my potential goes to waste rotting in your class. I thought I'd never get caught. I was a professional felon, like *Top Cat*. Then they sent a letter threatening to kick me out of school. A little extreme, don't you think?

My mom transformed into *The Predator*. Her wrath shook the whole neighborhood. Trees were uprooted, the power went out, mail boxes burst into flames! It was even worse than when she found out I was sneaking out at night. For a couple semesters I'd gotten away with it. I'd sit outside on the curb around midnight. Then Jamie, my boyfriend, would pick me up. He was always late. Sometimes he would drive me all the way to his house in Pittsboro, which was forty minutes away, but that was risky. So mostly we'd just screw around in the car. I'd leave the front door cracked open so my parents wouldn't hear me come back in. One morning I came home and the front door was locked. What kind of mother would do that???

I waited outside with the cats. Shivering in the lawn chair, thinking, "if I survive this I should join the CIA because I can withstand torture!" I bet she wasn't even asleep. She was just waiting for the hours pass. At 7:00 on the dot, she appeared, in her bathrobe. I was "ripped to shreds" like in the Blondie song.

When someone yells at me, I can press a button and eject myself out of my body. I can do it when other things happen to me, too.

I look down on myself and think, "damn, that sucks for her!"

It's like a homemade K-Hole.

I walk to Bruttoposse and watch the hipsters pile in. Body odor, V-necks, Chelsea Boots hiding socks with holes. The DJ walks past me without saying hi. He hasn't talked to me since last week's party. His name is Giancarlo and he works for MTV. It sounds cooler than it is, because Italian MTV is just dubbed American MTV.

Giancarlo has always been nice to me. He'd let me dance behind the booth with him and sometimes gave me free drinks. Last week he asked if I had a condom he could use (for a date, he said, though I didn't believe him). I just so happened to have one Trojan safety-pinned to my necklace. Ever heard of Sid Vicious?

The next day he yelled at me (texted me in ALL CAPS) because he was "embarrassed" by the fact that the condom I gave him had a hole in it. How stupid do you have to be? I get a drink and head into the dance floor. I'll find someone new to talk to tonight.

10. FREAK ON A LEASH

"Paris is so romantic you'll die." My boyfriend is texting me constantly now that I'm away. I should go to Paris more often. I mean, I would, if I liked it. I came here for fashion week, which I thought would be the most glamorous thing to ever happen to me, but to be honest? I'm underwhelmed. Once you've had one fashion week you've had them all. This year I've sat through six fashion shows, worked backstage at three of them and been to dozens of fashion parties, several hosted by me. You think the whole thing will be life-changing but you get used to it faster than a middle schooler gets used to huffing glue. It's the same people on rotation. There's the Facehunter, there's Chiara Ferragni, there's Cavalli having a heart attack…only men's fashion week is worth it in the end. You know why. I thought going to a foreign fashion week would be different. It's the same here but stiffer.

"You're right, the Starbucks killed me!" I reply to him and turn my phone off. See how he likes that. He thought I was kidding when I said I'd spend the whole trip going from one Starbucks to the other. I've spent so much time at Starbucks I ended up in bed with a barista. He went down on me for like, an hour. French men are perfect for oral sex because they don't have to do anything special, just speak French into my pussy and I'll have a nice time.

Merci beaucoup!

I haven't seen the Eiffel Tower or any of that crap. Just Starbucks and nightclubs. I threw ice cubes at Alexander Wang when he tried to push me off of his couch. What's his problem? I was dancing on it, having a fabulous time, everyone was looking at me so he got jealous! This always happens when someone is successful but boring. They realize that outside of their workplace nobody really cares about all the work they've done. And they freak out. Find a therapist, don't take your problems out on me!

After the bouncers threw me out, I went to the bar Pete Doherty is supposed to hang out in, Stolly's. He wasn't there. So I went home with a Polish photographer. He took naked pictures of me on a floor and in a bathtub. He covered me in guacamole. When his film roll was finished he took his clothes off to reveal enormous balls. Like, something is wrong with them. I did it with him out of pity. The poor guy could be dying! They've got a drink at Stolly's called the "Scooby Snack." They wouldn't tell me what is inside of it. They said it's a secret recipe. It tastes like breakfast cereal to me.

Paris is more depressing than Milan. Everything is medieval. Everyone is dirty. I'm not saying they smell bad. I'm just saying they're dirty. And if me saying that offends any French people, well, I'm offended too, what about that? They should get over themselves, and admit that Italians are more sophisticated, for using bidets. Everyone in Paris is so indulgent, when they eat or drink or smoke or screw they seem like they're doing it for the last time. In Paris, the apocalypse is right around the corner. You better be skinny when you meet your fate.

I'm staying with my Russian friend. I met Zina at NABA, by the vending machines. She approached me and said, "I saw you naked on that party website." I liked her immediately. She followed me around like a puppy and accepted everything I said as the truth. Not because she's a pushover or loser or anything; just because she's probably seen more screwed up scenes than me. When I asked her what her dad does she said, "when I was little we'd drive around town and he'd let me wait in the car in front of people's houses while he beat them up." She knows better than to question things. "Every time I go home my mom makes me apples with honey and I always tell her, mom, I'm allergic to raw apples! And she always tells me to suck it up."

Zina always made me laugh, whether she intended to or not. She'd talk and talk and take me to places I couldn't afford. "I don't like this pasta do you wanna finish it?" She'd push plates of penne and gnocchi and rigatoni towards me at the café by the Duomo where I only splurge on cappuccinos and cigarettes.

"Thanks, but I don't eat pasta."

Just as I was getting used to the idea of her being my best friend, she moved to Paris. "Photography schools are no good in Milan," she told me. I think she meant, "the photography professor I'm obsessed with doesn't want me so I'm starting a whole new life." Fair enough. I don't know what she's doing in school. She's loaded and she's hot. She's got long hair, amazing boobs, a pretty face with sad Russian Doll eyes...she could be the Paris Hilton of the European art world. Or at least a really elegant pillhead.

She now lives in a luxurious apartment on the Champs Elysees. The past few days she's brought random people over and they all react the same way. They freak out, lose their minds, pull their hair, hyperventilate, ask frantically, *demand* to know how much she pays. If I were her I'd kick them out. But she tolerates everyone. She says, "I don't know, ask my parents." Being rich seems annoying. She refuses to buy furniture. Maybe she thinks it helps her seem poor but it only makes her place larger. Miles of marble. We eat and drink on the floor.

"Oh, crap." I spit out my olive oil.

"What?" She takes the shot of oil and then the shot of vodka. It's a trick she learned in Moscow, from girls who drink on empty stomachs.

"My boyfriend just texted me. He says he got me a gift."

"So?"

"So, I didn't get him anything?"

"Why should you? You're a girl."

The night I land, we meet up at a bar by my school. The Mayflower. It's hideous, but it's a safe space for us to talk close and touch knees. He's in a quiet mood. He's looking at me like he did that first time I met him. It gives me goosebumps. I can tell he's just waiting for me to finish my drink so he can take me home. I chug it. I should have ordered a shot of oil!

Without a word, he takes me to his bed. We start with the usual stuff-he chokes me, slaps me, spits on me. I cry out. He says, "this is nothing, baby. We are playing like kids." What does he mean by that? "Are you ready for your gift?" He asks, standing up.

"Yeah," I say, catching my breath. "I'm ready."

He reaches under the bed to reveal a black plastic bag. It looks and sounds heavy. He hands it to me. "Take it out." I reach inside and feel leather and metal. I pull it out like a rattle snake. He got me a leash.

"Try it on."

I wrap the thick leather around my neck and struggle to close it. He clasps it shut for me, too tight. I guess it's pretty chic, if you think about it. Very Mugler. I ask how I look. He says, "like a whore."

He pulls the leash and it knocks the wind out of me. I fall

off the bed. Once I'm on my hands and knees, he pulls me towards the stairs.

"I treat my dogs badly," he says.

Cosmopolitan Magazine never taught me how to get dragged down the stairs properly. Is there a sexy way to do it? Ow! Ow! Ow! Ow! Thump! Thump! Thump!

I'm a pile of limbs at the bottom of the steps. Like a puppet without the hand inside of it. Before I can catch my breath, he drags me into the bathroom, kicks me to the ground and shoves my head in the toilet. He starts to do me doggy style. What's he so angry about? What have I done? He pulls on the leash so my head hangs inside the toilet, just above the water. If I move I'll drown! Thank god he has a maid and this thing is pretty clean. He finishes on my back. Then he pulls me up to my feet and tells me to get in the shower. Finally, some relief. Just kidding. He turns the water on, cold.

"Get on your knees, bitch."

He starts peeing.

"Drink it."

Well, I've had worse. Have you ever tasted Appalachian moonshine?

11. LA PORTA DELL'INFERNO

Being a Door Girl in a fashion capitol is like being the cheerleader in an American high school. Everyone resents you but has no choice but to be nice to you. You hold the keys to their social success. And you have an excuse to dress slutty. It's the coolest thing that ever happened to me.

Being a successful door girl is about the right mix of stamina and skills. Standing outside in the freezing cold, in high heels and underwear, bored out of your mind, having to make conversation with bouncers, is tough. But that's not the hardest part. The most difficult door girl-ing task is rejecting people. "Sorry, love, may I suggest the club next door? Or the McDonald's?" It doesn't come naturally to me. I hate when my anxiety gets in the way of being a cunt.

The club opens and the sea of leeches rush towards me. They'd tear me apart if they could. I feel like a witch at the stake. My clipboard of names is my shield. My cigarette is my sword. I smoke two packs a shift. I'm out here from 23:00. I'm allowed to go upstairs at 2:30. The party lasts till 5:00. Then I wait for my boss to get paid. Then we all go to an after-party! IT'S NOT A LIFESTYLE UNLESS IT'S KILLING YOU!!!

The types of people I let in:

1. Anyone on the list!! Duh.
2. Models I've gone out with.
3. Models I want to go out with.
4. My boss's friends who aren't on the list. They're easy to recognize-they're wearing Ferragamo and have frozen faces.
5. Well-dressed Russians.
6. Badly-dressed Russians. (Ugly clothes are the most expensive.)
7. Kids who have come several times, been rejected, and keep coming back. Patient, polite and persistent! It helps if they're cute, too.

The types of people I *don't* let in:

1. Drunk sfigati.
2. Sober sfigati.
3. Americans.
4. Beggars. I don't mean homeless people; I'd let them in instantly! But they don't come to my parties. I mean people who beg to be let in. Come up with a story, at least! Say you left your baby inside! Get creative, I'm SO bored out here!
5. Marangoni students. Hahahahhah!!! Fuckers.
6. My boyfriend.

Oh, cazzo. What's he doing here?

He's wasted. I guess he was at the strip club. He knows I work Friday nights. He stumbles towards me and gets up in my face.

"I wanna fuck your ass, bitch!"

"Ok, babe, let's talk later."

"Let me in, slut!"

The bodyguard asks if he's bothering me. I say yes. Well, he is! Sorry! I don't show up to *his* job saying I wanna fuck *his* ass! I tell the bouncer to handle him and I go to the bathroom to do blow.

I'm getting so wasted lately I didn't realize I was roofied. I only found out because Flow got roofied too. She called to tell me the story. Saturday night we ended up in the VIP area of... Plastic? Hollywood? Amnesia? The artist visiting from... London? Paris? Kentucky? paid for the table and the bottles. A friend told Flow that the artist was overheard saying, "I want all these girls fucked up." Flow and me were "all these girls." Good band name. A friend told Flow that the artist was seen pouring something into the drinks. Who is this "friend"? Why didn't they warn us at the time? I'm not one to criticize free drugs but these weren't fun. I couldn't stand or see so I crawled from one end of the club to the other, then I blacked out and then I woke up in my bed with my shoes on. I'm staying in bed today. My life depends on it.

"Are you OK?" I ask Flow.

"I'm better. What a ride!"

"That's what we get for being cute."

"What?"

"Ugly girls have to pay for their drugs. Pretty girls get roofied."

"Oh, Mia."

Oh me is right. My boss is in London, thank god. I can do flyers and mailing lists from home. The trick to doing work when hungover is covering one eye with your hand. It balances everything when you're seeing double. I love going on Facebook when I'm feeling bad because whatever's on there will make me feel better. An ex got fat, another got a teenager pregnant. Oh, my god! Is that...Frank? Writing to me? I must be hallucinating.

"Miao, Mia!"

"Ciao, Fra."

"Che fai?"

"Nothing, you?"

"Nothing. Come to my place."

Is this a prank? Is this a high school movie? Did he get dared to pretend to like me so that he can trick me into thinking it's real and everyone will find out and make fun of me? And he'll be like, "sorry, Mia, I only asked you out as a *joke*." And I'll be like, "well I'm sorry too, because I was only *ugly* as a joke!" And then I'll take off my glasses and let my hair down and be stunning. But I don't wear glasses or have long hair so what you see is what you get.

"So?" He writes me again when I don't respond to the last message.

I'M GOING TO SCREAM!!!! I scream.

"When? Now?" I reply.

"Sure."

"Where do you live?"

He gives me an address and I search it on Google. It's right by the freaking Duomo. Do people live there??? I dissolve a couple Aspirin in tap water and get dressed. I've got bruises all over my body from all the aspirin I take. Thin blood, thick skin. The trick to taking a tram when hungover is to focus on one spot ahead of you. Don't look outside the window, you will get dizzy. You will die! Look at someone's forehead wrinkle, someone's hairy mole, someone's hard nipple. You will survive this, you must. This is bigger than you. This is for history. HERstory! This is for all the women in your bloodline who came before you. This is for the ancestors who suffered unimaginable hardships just so one day their successors wouldn't have to. They did all of it so that you could fuck Frank.

He looks even better in the daylight. He's an off-duty vampire. His cheekbones stab me in the heart. His long hair is stringy and messy. He's wearing an unbuttoned white shirt and boxers. He smells like leaves and smoke. He lets me inside and shows me around. His apartment is monstrous in size. How many families live here? He takes me to a bed and throws me down. He reaches for my panties and I push him away.

I wear panty liners every day. The super thin "daily" pads most women wear when spotting. I hate discharge, I hate feeling it in my underwear, I hate knowing that I have it. A gyno told me that it's unhealthy to wear panty liners every day and I said it's unhealthy to not mind your own business. Being a woman is disgusting enough as it is. I don't wear them at night when I know I'm gonna screw. I must have been too messed up to register where I was going today. I was on Auto-Pilot. What an idiot! Frank seeing my pantyliner is a fate worse than death.

I accidentally pushed him to the other side of the bed. Roofies must be mixed with steroids. I tell him I need to use the bathroom and I'll be right back! But he's pissed now, in Italian. He's standing up. Has he never been rejected before, not even for a moment?

He shows me out. Just like that. Slams the door in my face. What just happened? I feel like an actress who blew her one audition with Sorrentino. I'm "the girl who didn't go to Paris" on *The Hills*. Now I know what it feels like to be the chick who says "NO."

My ancestors roll in their graves.

12. MIA MIU

My boss says she needs new shoes for tonight's party. I say I need new shoes for my whole life. She says let's get out of here, turns off the lights, runs down the stairs and leaves me in the dark.

"Wait, what?"

"Mia! Are you deaf or dumb?"

"Coming!!!"

I slam my laptop closed and shove it into my purse. I nearly trip down the stairs to catch up with her. Why are small women in such a rush all the time? She drives us to Monte Napoleone. She's got this gigantic Range Rover. It's way too big for her and completely ridiculous in general. She only has it because she's doing work for the brand. I guess you can't turn down a free car, regardless of how dumb it looks. I've only been on this street a few times, when we hosted special parties for design week or fashion week or who cares week. We pass Dolce, Prada, Gucci, all those guys. I know we aren't stopping in any of those places. I know her brand. Miu fuckin' Miu. Like Prada for baby hookers.

The theme of tonight's party is "DISCO SUCKS." Lately she's been letting me pick. Because she believes in me or because she's sick of doing it herself. Either way, I'm thrilled. I've done "Goth Goddess," "Rowdy Rednecks," "Gym Rats" and "Chaos in the UK." I get to make the flyers, too!

If I could afford to shop at any store, it would be this one. I "respect" brands like Vivienne Westwood and Yohji Yamamoto but I would never wear that stuff, it's too serious. Miu Miu makes clothes for tramps. For my boss and me. She tries on every pair of heels in the place and eventually chooses the first pair she tried on. That always happens, doesn't it? They're sparkling silver platform sandals. Like disco balls for your feet. In them she's as tall as me. She catches me staring at them in the mirror, in longing.

She's like, "You don't need designer stuff in your twenties."

"I know," I say, not convinced.

"Stick with me and you'll be buying Miu Miu one day!"

"Yeah. Or I could get a sugar daddy."

"Don't say that."

"Why not?"

"It's nasty."

"Or necessary."

"Don't play this game. I don't like your provocations."

"The things I say aren't provocative, they're true."

"Well, people will use your truth against you."

"How can they use the truth *against* me if I'm not *ashamed* of it?"

"You *should* be ashamed of some things, Mia."

"Like what!"

"Like…why all those naked photos?"

I want to say, "because I'm younger and cooler than you!" But instead I say, "nothing is embarrassing if you aren't embarrassed!"

She says something under her breath, like, "You're impossible," and walks away with her shoes on. I guess she's still annoyed about the other night.

We had dinner with an artist friend from London.

Someone she thinks is "important," no doubt. It's hard to keep track of who she thinks is "important" and who she thinks is "phony" because one often becomes the other in a matter of weeks. Anyway, this guy was really gorgeous, with transparent skin and bulging arms. I noticed he had squishy emerald green veins popping out everywhere. They were remarkable. So I made some quip about how easy he'd be to shoot up. He was like, "Oh my god, have you shot up?" And I said, "Oh my god, have you *not?*" He was like, "That's horrible!" And I was like, "Well, you're eating veal, so can *you* really say what's horrible?"

I come over later than I promised. I got caught up at a dinner with another boy I'm seeing. Gil is from Mexico. Him and his best friend Juan have both been with me. Once we had a threesome but it was too much work so I prefer to see them individually. Gil pumped me full of red wine at a steak restaurant. My boyfriend isn't happy.

"Next time don't come at all."

"Dn't say thaaat!" I'm trying not to slur.

"I don't like when you're drunk."

"We drnk togther evry nigh, silly!"

"It's different when you drink *with me*."

"Omgod, I'm ssso sorrrrry!"

"You need to drink less and eat more. You need strength to be a good slave."

"I AM good!" I fall while taking my shoes off.

"Take all your clothes off and crawl to me."

"Yez, sssir."

Crawling is easier than standing at this point. He's sitting on the sofa with his boner in one hand and my leash in the other. He puts it around my neck and pushes me into a deep-throat. I gag like a virgin. I push my head up against his hand and break away from his dick with just enough time to swallow the wine that spilled into my mouth from my stomach. A few drops spill out onto his pants. I look up at him. He's livid.

"Go downstairs. Lay on the bathroom floor and wait for me."

I'm good at waiting.

"I'm so sorry, Mia! I fell asleep on the couch! Your crying woke me up!"

I didn't realize I was crying.

"How did you stay here so long? Why didn't you come up and get me?"

I don't know how much time passed.

I shrug, and say, "You told me to wait."

He lifts me up off the floor and hugs me. He apologizes again. I say it's OK. He puts me in the shower, under hot water. He says, "You deserve a reward for your behavior." So he pees on me.

He dries me off, takes off my leash and curls up with me in bed. He falls asleep instantly. I take my phone out.

"I thought I was submissive in bed but it turns out, I'm just lazy."

He starts snoring. My chances of sleeping are slim. The snoring isn't the main problem. It's the radio. He has one next to the bed and keeps it on all night. Not silky jazz or ambient noises. He lets people, late-night radio hosts, talk him to sleep. I asked him one night if we could turn it off and he said I could leave if I wanted to. I haven't mentioned it since. One time at PRAVDA he told me he wishes there were more audio porn available, that he could play in his car. He said, "maybe you can make some for me." I said, "I have a bad voice."

I get out of bed and go to the bathroom. It seems so harmless now. It's just a bathroom. Hours ago it was prison. There's a perfume bottle on the counter. *Lola* by Marc Jacobs. That's my scent. Did I leave it here? No, he doesn't let me leave stuff in the bathroom. Did he buy it for me? No. It's half used. Hmmm...I notice other things around that weren't there before. A comb—that definitely can't be his. Haha! Oh, my god. No. It's HER. Her stuff! The move-in is already happening. Gradually and dreadfully.

13. L'ANIMA DELLA FESTA

At night Milan lights up like a cigarette you found on the ground. Filthy and miraculous. The buildings are deformed and malnourished. People walking by are on edge. They're holding in pee and late for a movie. Amateur graffiti hangs around glumly. "Porco Dio" and random names of boys I've probably kissed. They should teach graffiti at NABA. My mom says Milan is the most dangerous city in Europe. I say that's because of me!

People who think parties are trivial have never been to a good party. A good party is a spiritual experience. You come to worship the God of FUN! And when you let that God into your crummy heart, you're free. Most people who want to "escape society" go on top of a mountain or into a desert or... Sardegna. They don't get it. You can only "escape" society by fucking society in the ass and we all know you can only fuck an ass by diving in, ruthlessly.

A party is the closest you can get to pooping in the middle of a crowded street and getting away with it. Nobody gives a shit if you shit in the desert. When the music gets loud I scream bloody murder and nobody cares because they think I'm singing. I can throw myself on the floor in protest of life itself and look like I'm dancing. I can cry, vomit, steal, push, spit, step on feet, black out, wake up and do it all over again. You can live your whole life at a party, an alternate life where the only rules that apply are applied to your outfit. And here's my rule about that: if you don't like what you're wearing, take it off!

The secret to a good party is elusive. You can have everything: stunning setting, open bar, dream playlist, hot guests, Kate Moss doing lines off of Naomi Campbell's abs, a line of cover boys waiting for you in the bathroom. But that doesn't mean the party will be good. If something is missing, everyone can feel it. But not everyone can fix it! Someone has to rip off the Band-Aid and get the party started. Someone has to add the sprinkle of magic, the personal touch. Most people can't be bothered to do that. They're wearing their outside personalities. They need someone to shake them out of it. That someone is me.

But anyone can be The Life of the Party. Here's how:

1. MOOD: Spread whatever emotion you come in with. Don't keep anything inside. You're depressed? Share the sadness! Sure, it's best to be happy-or excited-at a party. Smiles fit better, aesthetically. But nobody is really happy. That's why we do drugs! The important thing is to get away from the polite "small-talk" of regular every day being. The "how are you?" "I'm OK" stuff. At a party when someone asks, "how are you?" say, "I'll show you!" Then take your tampon out and throw it at them.

2.ROLE: You must decide your "party persona" and devote yourself to it. The show starts when everyone plays their part. Are you the fashion victim? The slut? The DJ? The groupie? The VIP? The wannabe? The dancer? The loser? The junkie? The loner? The center of attention? The mess? The cop? The asshole? The pervert? Choose honestly and act accordingly.

3. GIFTS: What do you have to offer? Gossip? Coke? Your body? GIVE IT UP!

4. GOALS: What are you trying to accomplish at this party? What steps must you take to reach this goal? You want to steal someone's boyfriend? You want to have pictures taken of you? You want to hide in a corner and talk to the voices you hear in your head? Don't let anyone stop you!

5. MOVEMENT: Throw yourself around like the piece of garbage you are! I'm an awful dancer but that doesn't matter. You just have to do it HARD. Pretend you're possessed by Satan. Or actually get possessed, for real. MDMA helps.

6. CONFIDENCE: I know you don't really like yourself but if you pretend that you do, other people will believe it and after a few drinks you'll believe it, too. (You'll feel twice as bad the next day for doing so—borrowing endorphins you don't have —but that's something to worry about tomorrow.)

7. EYE CANDY: Caring about your looks will ruin your night. The minute you hit the dance floor you should forget all the mirrors and pictures that distorted your perception of self. Being ugly is powerful. Youth in itself is beautiful. Everyone wants it! So actually, when you're young, you should do your best to be as ugly as possible. When you're old you can look nice (if you're still alive).

8. EFFORT: Don't give a damn! Sometimes nothing is worth it. Sometimes, the best thing to do to a party is to leave it.

"WHAT IS THIS A CLUB OR A CHURCH?"

The bouncer throws me to the curb. I spit at his feet as he walks away.

"I'M NEVER COMING BACK TO THIS DUMP!"

My boyfriend took me to a concert at Plastic. Nobody was paying enough attention to me so I jumped on stage. The band loved me. I danced around with them and someone from the crowd handed me a rose. The crowd loved me. Then the bouncer came and grabbed me, so I shoved the rose in his face. I'd make him love me. He picked me up and started dragging me off stage. I kissed him on the mouth. He threw me into the crowd. They cheered. I climbed back on stage. The bouncer picked me up, cradled me like a baby, carried me outside and threw me into the street.

My boyfriend was ignoring me because he was busy sucking up to some "important" work friend. How important can a grown man who wears a backpack be? How am I getting home? Oh, good. My boyfriend came out. He looks pissed.

"Mia. Why you always make a merda?"

"I was just bored."

He pushes me against a tree and puts a hand on my neck.

"How you can be bored with me?"

"You weren't paying attention!"

He puts the other hand on my neck.

"I always pay attention."

He kisses me and chokes me so hard I can't breathe.

Men are obsessed with strangling. I spent my sixteenth birthday alone in a bookstore. I met a college guy there. He said he had been watching me for an hour and wanted to know what I was doing. I said I was celebrating my birthday and buying some books. He asked for my phone number and I said there's no point giving it to him, since I have a boyfriend. He said, "Why isn't your boyfriend with you on your birthday?" I said, "He doesn't care about that kind of stuff." He was like, "You mean he doesn't care about *you*?" I was like, "I donno." So he said, "You deserve better," and I was like, "I guess." He said, "I wanna show you something," so I followed him to the back of the bookstore. He said let's sit on the floor.

He said, "Your neck is so graceful, I'd love to choke you." And then he choked me in the children's section of the bookstore. I only managed to get up because some people walked by and saw us.

Then I ran out and called Jamie. He wanted to know the guy's name, how he looked, what school he attended. I was like, why?

The next day Jamie and his friends found the guy and beat him with baseball bats. I saw him a couple weeks later, walking towards me on Franklin St. He had a broken arm in a cast. He crossed the street when he saw me.

It's not his fault I have such a gorgeous neck. There's something about it, you just wanna grab it! My grandmother picked me up by my neck when the war alarms started in Sisak. She carried me by the gullet, like a chicken headed for slaughter. In my case, we were fleeing down to the basement. I watched my feet dangle above the steps for five stories. I think that's the moment my tonsils started exploding in size. The combination of fear, strangulation and alarms created a freak reaction. Land mines in my throat.

He lets go before I pass out. I swallow.

"You going back inside?" I ask.

"Are you allowed back inside?"

"Probably not. No."

"So let's go home." He puts his arm around me and we walk towards a taxi stop.

So that's all it takes to get some attention?

14. BLACK COFFEE

Italian coffee culture is to blame for everything: Berlusconi's tan, the financial crisis, Prada's painful shoes, the mafia's brutal murders, the inane programming on Rai2. For a nation of people who care so much about the stuff you put in your bodies, how can you explain such a tragedy?

Sit your Emporio Armani jeans wearing ass down. Why do you stand while you drink your coffee? Who are you, a teen girl taking her first shot of tequila at a sports bar? What are you in a rush for? Y'all are late to everything! Why pretend to acknowledge the concept of time during the single part of the day that should be savored? Who are you trying to fool? Not me!

Croatians sit with their coffee, like civilized people. We take our time and chain-smoke cigarettes. The unemployed Croatians sit with their coffee until it's time to sit with a beer. Americans do the same thing, only replace the cigarettes and beer with donuts and French fries. French people are so obsessed with sitting at their café's I bet all their bony butts are covered in sores. When I complain about this coffee problem my Italian friends are like, "we don't really *do* breakfast." As if that's something to be proud of.

Well, here's an idea: what if you stop having such enormous, extravagant, late night dinners? Maybe then you won't wake up so full that all you can stomach is a sip of orange juice and a splash of espresso in the face. Also, hello: coffee isn't just for breakfast! It's an anytime-anywhere-any reason thing. "When we want to sit and talk with our friends we have aperitivo." So? Alcohol and coffee have nothing to do with each other. That's like someone asking me, "why are you walking around barefoot?" And me answering by pointing to my hat! PS: You can take your Spritz and wash my dishes with it because it tastes like soap.

Since y'all love standing with your coffees I'd assume you'd enjoy walking with them as well. There is not a single to-go cup in the entire country. A STYROFOAM CUP WITHOUT A LID DOES NOT COUNT. Even if you did have to-go cups, what would you put in them? A few lousy drops of espresso? A deflated cappuccino (that you can legally only order before noon)? Have you people never felt the bliss that is clutching a paper cup with the girth and warmth of kitten, as you pace the streets, like Mary Kate Olsen on her way to rehab?

At least your brioches are good. I'll admit it. I'm sharing one with the pigeons in the park across the street from Gattullo. I don't know if I can call it a park. It's just a couple benches in a patch of grass near the taxis. Gattullo is a "historic" café, meaning it's full of widows, veterans and media hipsters. I'm looking at apartments in the area. I'm trying to picture myself having coffee there every morning, rubbing shoulders with bitter Sciure and the types of men who would try to explain my own name to me if they got a chance.

"Hey pigeons how's life on this street?"

One pigeon is old and blind, the other is young and shiny.

"Not bad. You've got a pharmacy, a tobacco bar, a tram stop and taxis."

"And I've got you guys!"

"If you keep the brioches coming." The young one winks at me.

I can't wait to move. I hate sneaking around Maria. Just because we used to be close, like a whole YEAR ago, she thinks she can have some say about my new life. She's so judgmental. And she's trying to make me feel guilty about leaving. She's like, "This is such a small space, who else can I share it with?" I'm like, I don't know, maybe if you had more friends it wouldn't be such an issue. I refuse to feel guilty! Of course she doesn't want me to go—I'm an invisible roommate, she has the place to herself. And yet, she suffocates me. She says she's "worried" about me. She should worry about herself. Mind your own business. My new roommate will be the opposite of Maria. I met her at an after-party. She's from Paris. She's nuts.

"Call the realtor and ask for a date. If you fuck him he'll lower the rent," she says, lighting a joint.

"Um...that seems risky? And he's gross."

"Come on! I would do it, but I have a boyfriend." Her accent kills me.

"So do I!"

"Yeah? I thought he was somebody's husband?"

Damn, she's good.

After what happened with Frank, things actually got better between us. Can you believe it? He likes me *more* now. I think he might even "respect" me? I'll never understand straight men. Nothing they do makes sense. Anyway, the bad news is I don't think he'll ever try to hook up with me again. The good news is: (are you ready) (are you sure?) the good news is, the good news is (!!!) the good news is he wants to SHARE his birthday party with ME! That's pure Sagittarius love, dude!

He made a Facebook event about it. We're hosting it at his famous Cunt Club party, which I've been going to for two years now, even before I became so pathetically popular. If you had told me this back when I used to go to CC by myself, I would have thrown a drink in your face and called you a liar. And now the event has MY NAME attached to it. Is this what celebrities feel like when they become famous? Is this my "moment?" Am I peaking? Let's be honest, I peak every night. Will my whole life go downhill from here? Probably. Who cares!

My boyfriend isn't impressed. He was hoping we'd hang out alone. Hah, in his dreams. He's like, "This is one of our last nights alone," and I'm like, "Not if you leave her!" OK I didn't actually say that, I'd never say that, I'm afraid to.

I'm stopping by his place before my party, just for a birthday kiss. I don't have time to waste. I'm wearing all of my nicest stuff and…I got a NEW BLACKBERRY. Yes, dude! My mom got it for my birthday. Well, she had to send me money and let me buy it for myself, because the last time she tried to send me a package the post office stronzi stole it. Another time she sent me a package it was sent back to her. Vaffanculo, la Posta Italiana.

My Blackberry is my new boyfriend. I'm in love with him. And that's not all. My mom also got me Lady Gaga concert ticket as a Christmas present! (My birthday and Christmas are less than a week apart, a curse and a blessing, thank you Jesus). I've been dying to see this icon perform, it's her first world tour, and I think she's the next David Bowie. So my plan is to have the most amazing 24 hours of my life. Tonight, I'm going to be a star, I'll stay out all night, take loads of drugs, not sleep, go straight home to change into my Gaga look and then go straight to the show. Hi, have we met? I'm Mia, the luckiest troia alive!

"I'm here!" I walk in like I'm closing the goddamn Victoria's Secret runway.

"Hey, baby." He's slouching at the dining table, in the dark. Glum.

"Is this for me?" I straddle him and pick up the bottle of vodka on the table.

"Happy birthday."

"Wow, this gift is...perfect!"

"I'd prefer to buy you a drink at our swinger's bar, but since you're busy..."

"But you could come tonight! It will be fun!"

"I doubt it."

"Come ON!"

"I'll keep my door unlocked until midnight."

He rubs his hands on my thighs, slowly moving up.

"What?"

"After that, find somewhere else to sleep."

I laugh. "Oh, babe, you think I'd come back by then? There's NO way it will be over that early, unless something horrible happens. Like the apocalypse! The party doesn't even *start* until then!"

He reaches my crotch, pulls the at my tights and rips a hole the size of a fist.

"Che cazzo hai fatto! These are my best tights!"

"Good."

"And it's freezing outside!"

"Now you'll think about me all night."

I'll think about my tights all night, dickhead. Fatal Fifty is their name. They're 50 denier seamless black Wolford tights with an elastic waistband. I got these for myself as a birthday gift. These cost more than my dresses, more than my shoes. What a jerk.

"Come downstairs, bitch," my gorgeous Blackberry delivers the message.

Flow and Cat and some other girls are on the street waiting for me. Thank god. I grab my bottle and walk out, fuming.

Flow is like, "what's wrong" and I'm like, "nothing!" Nothing is wrong. I'm determined to have fun tonight.

Everyone is here. Our mutual friends, my boss, my boys, my enablers. Frank, of course. Even Maria is here, against her better judgement. It's nice. But it's also not…*that* nice. It's just…like any other party. Only, at this party, people expect me to smile. "Hey, cheer up, it's your birthday!" Is this how it feels when you get what you want? It feels like nothing?

"I wanna open you up like a peach," my Blackberry glows.

What does that even mean? If he thinks I'm going to spend my birthday party texting him, he has mental problems.

I have a few hundred drinks and check my phone a few hundred times. He texts me again at midnight.

"Last chance to come over."

My vagina is freezing her ass off. I need to keep my stamina up. I'm bored to death. Nobody cares about me. They're just acting like it's any other party on any other day. There's no cake and no bags full of powder with my name on them. Whatever. The FB event speaks for itself and it will be there forever: proof that I made it! And anyway, it's actually fine if tonight is a disappointment because tomorrow will be legendary.

When the sun comes up I go home. I shower and re-do my makeup. I put on the long, blonde wig my boss lent me. I slip into the black leotard my boss gave me (it's Top Shop from London). I step into my highest heels, from Zara, shaped like Louboutins. I throw away my ruined tights, hold a funeral service, say kind words, pay my respects, shed a tear. I throw on my fur coat and call a taxi. I realize I have no idea where this stadium is. Good thing I brought a hundred bucks. There it all goes.

I'm so early. Hours early. Everyone is waiting in line for their spot in the monster pit. I don't have monster pit tickets, but that's ok. I probably have a cute seat. I just have to walk around until doors open so I don't freeze. Milanese winter is vicious. It's not white fluffy romance. It's grey, pitiless poison. I walk in circles. I find a bottle of champagne next to a parked car. I pop it open and drink it by myself. Some local news station asks to interview me. I spit champagne at the camera. They yell stuff at me. I yell stuff at them. I sit in a pile of leaves and try to surf the web on my Blackberry. It's slow.

I drink more.

Finally, it's time to go in. I've finished my bottle so I'm just drunk enough to mask my hangover from last night. I'm struggling to keep my eyes open. My wig is tangled, my makeup is smeared. I'm ready for the show! This is my first arena concert. This is my first pop concert. I've only ever been to small venues before, to see bands like The Casualties, Anti-Flag, Leftover Crack, angry teen stuff. I'm in for a treat. I'll have a luxurious seat with a great view. Sophisticated adult stuff!

What the shit is this shit? Why do people go to arenas? My seat is in the nosebleed section. Like, there is nothing behind my seat. Behind me is a wall. I've got the highest possible seat. My mom said it costs 70 Euros, how is that possible? I can't sit comfortably. My legs are so long with these heels on that they don't fit in the small space provided. When I stand up I've got to stay straight with my back pressed against the wall, otherwise I'll fall into the abyss of the crowd beneath me. I can't see Lady Gaga because I didn't bring my glasses and I can't hear Lady Gaga because everyone next to me is screaming their heads off and they don't even know the lyrics. I…hate my life.

"Where are you?"

Hah! Look who's texting me first today!

"I'm at the Gaga concert, remember?" I must have told him a million times.

"Me too. Where are you seated?"

What? The fuck?

"I'm in…the highest seat, you?"

"I'm front row."

WHAT THE FUCK.

"That's..amazing! Can I join you?"

"No, babe."

Ok, nooooo freaking way. How dare he! He knows I love Lady Gaga. And he doesn't give a crap about her. He's never heard any of her songs! He doesn't even let me talk about her for more than five minutes! And now he's HERE! And he's here with HER! And they have GREAT SEATS! And he's TELLING ME ABOUT IT?! Every single thing about this is so wrong Oprah would need a week to cover it on her show. What's his problem? Is this some sick joke? Does he hate me?

"I'm SO happy for you BOTH." I shove my phone into my pocket and then remember that my fur coat has a hole in both pockets. So I just hold it there.

The only thing that would make this fair is if my body lands on their heads when I throw myself down the stairs. But I don't do that because this is my boss's wig and she'd kill me if something happened to it.

I imagined I'd cry at this concert but not because of them. The show is finally over and I didn't enjoy a second of it. I have to get out of here so I can say goodbye to the worst day of my life in the peace of my bed. I make it through the stampede only to find there are no taxis. We're in the middle of nowhere and I have no clue how I'm getting home.

"Hey, Mia?"

No. Please Please Please don't be—

"Oh my god! Hi!"

This is the first time I've seen her in person. I can't believe that this is who he's choosing. She's thin and she has a good rack. But she's not beautiful. Not even close. Her face is bare and her hair is deflated. Her style is horrendous. This is what they call "Radical Chic" in Italy. A style that translates to "I dress so that people know I watch the news." When I look at her I only see distressed denim and rage. The rage is mine, blocking my vision. I have to admit the two of them complement each other. They make sense. But I refuse to accept it!

"Mia, do you want a ride?" my boyfriend asks, sheepishly.

DON'T TALK TO ME ASSHOLE! YOU'RE DEAD TO ME!

"I'm fine, thanks."

What the hell is he thinking? And what is *she* thinking? Does she know? Or is she stupid? Everyone knows, so she must. But if she did, why isn't she grabbing my wig off my head and trying to hang me with it? I don't know what I would hate more about her. If she were totally oblivious or "cool with it." I guess it's worse if she's cool with it because that means I don't matter. I guess I don't matter either way.

"How are you getting home?" she asks.

"I don't know. I'll wait for the crowd to go down at this Spizzico. I have a Blackberry now so I can surf the web."

"That's silly, just come with us," she says.

I would rather do anything else, you troll from hell! I'll stay in the Spizzico tonight and wait for everyone to leave. Then I'll fall asleep under a table. Tomorrow morning, I'll ask for a job. I'll spend my adult years here, making square pizzas. I'll grow old and retire. After my last shift, I'll buy a bottle of champagne. I'll drink it where I found the champagne bottle today. I'll smash the bottle on the curb and slit my wrists with the glass.

"Nah, I'll call a taxi."

"No taxis will come out here! Don't be stupid," he says.

But I AM STUPID! Haven't you gotten to know me after all this time you've been screwing my body and screwing my brain and screwing my life up?!

I climb into the back of their stupid car. They sit silently in the front like parents. I clear my throat.

"I didn't know you guys were Gaga fans," I say.

"We're not, the tickets were gifted."

Ugh, I wasn't talking to *you*, cunt.

"How lucky! Did you love it?"

"She was fine," she says, with a shrug.

FINE? This *stronza* just called the new genius of our generation *fine*? And she got to be in the front row? This is beyond unfair. This is pure injustice. This is spiritual massacre. This is like when a rich person can buy any clothes they want but they choose to wear earth tones.

That's it, no more conversation. Thank god I've got my Blackberry to keep me company. The only way this hour-long car ride will go well is if we get into a fatal accident. I hope they've been drinking.

So here's the story. They've been together since college. They got married young. Then they had a big fight. He didn't say what it was about, but knowing him, it was his fault. The fight was so big that she left him. She moved away to another town. She got a new job, started a new life, started seeing other people. Then, about six months ago, after I met him, she changed her mind.

"She showed up at my door, crying and begging me to take her back."

"And what did you say?"

That morning I'd grasped for any sign of hope. Hanging onto his pillow as if it were the edge of a cliff.

"I said, OK." He laughed, as if he just told me a dumb blonde joke.

But, he explained, before she could move back in with him she had to wait for her contract to end at work. Career woman. Respect. No problem, I thought. Before that happens, he'll fall in love with me and he'll tell her it can't work out. Or they'll fight again, for whatever reason. When a couple fights once they'll fight again. There are endless bad things that can happen before then. Just rest assured that something bad will happen. I got what I wished for. Something bad happened. This is it. Here we are.

15. NUOVO ANO STESSE PALLE

I'm staying in tonight. Maria is at her parent's place. I have the apartment to myself for a week before I move out. My boyfriend is with his wife. Do I look like I give a damn? I'll watch the entire *Aqua Teen Hunger Force* series on FreeTV.com and drink whiskey until I puke—or fall asleep.

"Come over, bitch," Flow texts me.

"Flow, leave me alone!" I say out loud but not to her.

"I know you're there!"

I'm not answering.

"Answer me!"

"I'm staying in tonight," I text back.

"But it's New Year's Eve!"

"That doesn't mean anything."

"It's sad to stay in tonight."

"It's sad to go out tonight."

I put my Blackberry under a pillow and get in the shower. I get off under the hot water. I think about that time we hooked up in this bathroom. He pushed me into this shower and tried to pee on me but couldn't, because he was too hard. So he pulled me out and picked me up and threw me around the bedroom I share with Maria. He had me until I begged for him to stop.

Simpler times.

I get into pajamas, the comfy ones my mom got me at the Gap. I prepare a tall glass of whiskey and a spoon full of Nutella. I'm ready for health, for self-love, for bliss. NEW YEAR NEW ME! FreeTV.Com is down again. Couch-Tuner.Com is flooded with pop-up ads and bad links. What, is everyone in the world at home trying to watch shows on streaming? Don't they have a party to go to? *PORCO CAZZO DIO CANE!* I reach under the pillow.

"What did you have in mind?"

"Party at mine."

"I'm not in the mood to go crazy," I text.

"It will be chill!" she replies.

She's lying. We're both lying to each other. This is the language of addicts. I used to think she was my "bad influence," the friend who brings the worst out of me. Then I realized I'm that for her, too. We all need someone blame for our own behavior.

"Who's coming?"

"Just friends!"

False! All our friends are with their families. Her and I are the only two povere puttane in town without anyone to care for us. This isn't going to be pretty. I'm actually scared. But I'm also thrilled. I don't think I can stoop lower than where I'm at now but I am eager and willing to try.

There's a thin line between "wholesome" to "wretched." People's entire lives can pivot on a decision like this: stay on the couch or go to the party? It's small decisions like this that make the difference between becoming a respected professor with a cozy home and loving family, or a crazy lady living in a cardboard box under a bridge by the highway with a pet rat.

"See you in an hour."

I chug my whiskey and get dressed.

. . .

She's already lit up like a firecracker. How much stuff has she taken? Can I have some? She's frantically moving things around, for who knows who.

"Do you want a pickle or something?"

Ever since she saw me drink all the juice from a pickle jar, (it's a Slavic trick to fight hangovers-and it's delicious) she never fails to offer me a treat when I come over.

"No thanks I had a spoonful of Nutella for dinner."

Someone knocks on the door. A dozen of the sketchiest people I've ever seen in my life pile in. Men over fifty and hookers our age.

I take her aside and ask, "who are these clowns?"

"Does it matter? They have drugs."

I lay on the couch between lines of speed and blow and MDMA. The oldest guy here sits at my feet. I'm guessing he's Flow's sugar daddy. He's been asking her about her rent and groceries and stuff like that. She's calling him Papi. Ok, now her apartment and her lifestyle make sense. He starts massaging my feet, then he works his way up my legs. Now he's under my skirt. He fondles me over my tights. It feels OK. Flow sees us and smiles.

We're all naked. The men want to go all the way but they have no condoms. We send them out to get some. Figurati if they can find any so late on NYE! We laugh at them, just us girls. We're already naked and turned on and now we're bored, too, so we do each other. We've got a purple dildo.

"Mia, you've got such a pretty body."

"Thanks, Flow."

We've been going down on each other for eternity. Why do men make this seem like a burden? It's so much easier than blowjobs.

"Girls!" The Nigerian hooker interrupts, excited.

"What?"

"HAPPY NEW YEAR!"

Oh, yeah. It's midnight. I've gotta text him!

I get up and walk to the bathroom. I look in the mirror and say, "Don't do this, you're high." Then I start laughing. Because, well, I'm high. *Just Do It.* "I know I can't say this but I love you." I text my boyfriend. I put the phone down on the sink and it buzzes immediately.

He texts me back. "Love you."

It's rude to say things you don't mean. I feel sick.

The men come back with soft dicks and no condoms. We do drugs until noon and I get a ride home from one of the dudes. He feels me up in the car while I hold vomit down.

I regret letting him know where I live.

When I open my door, I drop to the floor and start sobbing. I crawl into the shower. My body and ego are bruised. How long were we screwing around and what drugs did we use?

I've been in bed for days. I'm living off coffee, sparkling water with Aspirin, spoonfuls of honey and Facebook.

"Baby, I've been calling you."

"You and everyone else."

My boyfriend is messaging me on FB. I left my Blackberry in that guy's car on the way home from Flow's. Thinking about any second of that night makes me miserable so I would rather get a new Nokia than to try and retrieve it. Happy New Year to me!

Can you believe I have to go back to work tomorrow? I can't possibly fathom it. I would give anything-I mean, I would die-to be home watching cartoons. To have my mom bring me a bowl of cereal and tell me something nice. Before I went rotten. Why did I? I'm a merda. I'm a condom stuck under your shoe after using a public bathroom. I'm food smashed between your teeth that turns into a cavity. I'm black grit under your finger nails that gets pushed deeper into your skin when you try to pry it out. I'm a pimple you press before it's ready to be popped, becoming a large, throbbing sore, deforming your face. "What have I done?" You scream, "I should have left it alone!" I'm a toxic lip injection. I'm an eyelash that scratches your cornea. I'm an ingrown hair that collects pus. I'm the kind of filth that doesn't wipe away, you've got to use a whole roll of toilet paper to get me off and even then, you don't feel clean.

After me you need a shower.

"Don't be sad, baby. I'm thinking of you," he says.

I'm thinking of me too. And that's why I'm so sad. Screw him, screw everyone. I'm going back to sleep.

I have that dream I've been having periodically since I was little. I'm in an empty room covered in green moss. I'm small. I look around and see something on the opposite end, in a corner. I crawl towards it. It moves away as I crawl closer. The walls move away, too. I have to crawl fast! Eventually, I touch it, by stretching myself out on the ground and reaching my arms as far as they go. It's tiny but it's glowing. I've got it. It's a pink tube. A Labello lip balm. I roll it between my palms and feel warmth. I open it up and twist up the pink butter. I think, "now I have everything." Then I hear my own voice. It's surrounding me like thunder, pouring from the walls. "You are dreaming," it says. "When you wake up you'll have nothing." And then I wake up and have nothing. It's a stupid dream but I always wake up in a sweat. I open my computer and let the light purify me.

Twitter.com. *"I'm not saying I wish I were dead I'm just saying I wish I were never born and there is a difference."*

16. SHAMELESS

Only weak people suffer from embarrassment for more than a few moments. Anyone can talk themselves out of feeling embarrassed over farting loudly at a dinner or tripping in front of their crush on the sidewalk and knocking out their front teeth. Well-timed comedic misfortunes make the world go round.

Shame is different. Shame makes your organs hurt. It melts your feet into the pavement. It punches you in the soul. Shame is a mouse dying slowly in a trap because it wanted the cheese. As a teenager I didn't think I deserved a bed. It's something I haven't unpacked yet. But at 6:00 each morning I'd wake up on my bedroom floor or on the couch downstairs and I'd head into the kitchen. I'd make an overflowing bowl of cereal and take a large coffee mug out of the cupboard. I'd bring them both to the couch. While watching cartoons on mute, I'd chew the cereal and spit it into the mug. When the mug filled up, I'd take it to the toilet and flush it. Then everyone else would wake up and I'd get ready for school. I'd still be starving by then but my cheeks would be swollen like a chipmunk's. Once my mom came downstairs early.

"What are you doing?"

I couldn't look at her.

"I couldn't sleep. Having an early breakfast," my hand clenched the top of the mug so hard my knuckles turned white.

"What's in the mug?"

"Nothing."

"Mia, what's in the mug?"

"Mom, leave me alone."

"MIA, SHOW ME."

Shame keeps you up at night even after you're dead.

My boyfriend printed out a "limited edition" magazine, just of me. Foul things I've done on the street or in bathrooms, blackout drunk. Things I'd only do when I'd go out with the Banda and make a mess of myself. I didn't pose for these thinking I'd ever hold them in my hand. I hardly remember these moments, much less the camera flash. That's what I hate about photography. And photographers. They're leeches.

You can feel like doing something in one moment but that doesn't mean you want that moment to exist forever. What if someone took a photo of everything you've ever done? Would you want it in a magazine? Why would he do this?

I thank him for it, shove it in my purse and throw it away in a trash can on the street on my way home. I rip it to shreds, first. Screaming.

"I'm so sorry! I slept through my alarm!"

I never sleep through my alarm. We were supposed to meet at Gattullo this morning. We have to meet at inconvenient times now that she's back.

"I had to eat so many pastries without you."

I wanted to go but I couldn't because I was paralyzed. I cried in the bath until the water got cold. Yes, my new place has a bath tub. And if I had any self-respect I'd drown myself in it.

. . .

I'll live in a motel one day. Not a hotel. *Hotels* are for people with too much cash and no ambition. My motel will be by the side of a highway, sheltering people with purpose: truckers, hookers, immigrants, junkies, single mothers, runaways, me. I'll pay for my continued stay by cleaning the rooms. I'll prove myself irreplaceable by salvaging a scabies outbreak (Jamie and I got them once at a crackhouse). As a reward for my dedicated service I'll get promoted to reception. Once I've got that kind of power, I'll give special discounts to people in need and/or in cool outfits. I won't ask whores for their passports or judge the Johns they bring in.

I'll let a group of local teens loiter when they don't know where to go. "It's safer if you get high here than on the street." I'll serve them bowls of Froot Loops and Lucky Charms leftover from the continental breakfast. I'll let them watch the TV in the lobby. Using an ancient VCR I'll educate them on classic cinema: *Wayne's World, Beavis and Butthead Do America,* and *Detroit Rock City.* I'll give them a camera for Christmas (a pervert photographer forgot it in his room) and insist they make an art film. "But we got no money, no actors, no nothin'!" I'll tell them about the crap John Waters made in Baltimore before he got famous. "It was amateur, but people loved it. Just shoot something trashy here." I'll give them the master keys and say, "go crazy!"

I'll submit their film to festivals and it will be a hit. The motel will become a cult destination sensation. People from all over will come to see it! To celebrate our new guests, I'll pimp-out the breakfast buffet with an addition of homemade Burek, my mom's recipe. It's not that hard. You just need the right kind of cheese. Salty feta, I think. I'll only have access to gas station groceries so I'll make do with Philadelphia Cream Cheese. The profits will shoot through the roof and we'll renovate the rooms. Wallpaper with palm trees. Shaggy carpets and furniture from the 60's. Beaded curtains for every doorframe. When the owner dies, she'll leave the motel to me because at that point, I'm family.

Now that it's mine, I can put into reality the dream that I've had all these years. Every room comes with a pet. "Don't be silly, he won't sleep in your bed. He has his *own*, by the TV, see? Hey...where are you going?" The news will spread, grossly misinterpreted by the press. "Hotel Health Hazard." It's *a motel*, damnit. Guests will stop coming. The junkies and truckers are long gone; they were shunned by our cinema-snobs. Even my teen protégés moved away with scholarships to prestigious film schools. I'll spend my final days roaming the empty rooms with my pet rats, reminiscing about the past. "No regrets," they'll tell me.

"You should get 'No Regrets' tattooed," my boyfriend says.

I snap out of the daydream.

"It should be in cursive on your chest," he points between my boobs.

We're in a motel in Bologna. He has business here and invited me to come along. I guess I'm a real mistress now. We're having dinner downstairs in the restaurant.

"That's a stupid tattoo," I reply, pushing my salad around.

"All tattoos are stupid."

He isn't wrong. I've got a toaster on my wrist. It's from my favorite cartoon, *The Brave Little Toaster*. But nobody watches that here so when they see the ink they think I randomly love appliances.

The restaurant is decorated like the inside of a ship. The booths are made from planks found on barrels. There's a buffet of greasy vegetables and a tank with a live eel in it. I want to set her free. I'd smuggle her out around my neck. "What on earth are you accusing me of? This scarf is Givenchy!" I'd keep her alive on the train by spraying her with Chanel no.5. I can't wear *Lola* by Marc anymore. You know why. Then I'd throw her in the Naviglio. She'd be swamp queen.

He's eating pizza and I ordered caprese. He's particular about his food, too. He's only adventurous when it's exceptional. He ate tons of exotic shit when he lived in China—a period of his life he brings up often. But if a restaurant is beneath his standards he only dares to order pizza margarita. I've watched him eat a million of them by now. It's kind of hypocritical, if you ask me. When my caprese arrived he told me that he doesn't like sleeping with girls who eat cheese because it makes them "smelly." His pizza is full of cheese, so I guess the rule only applies to girls. As most rules do. He's drinking a pint of beer and I'm on my third martini.

"Have you been studying?" he asks.

"Ew, what? No."

"I don't go out with stupid girls."

"So you admit we go out now?"

"You want to be my girlfriend but if you were my girlfriend I'd dump you."

"Excuse me?"

"You misbehave too much, baby," he laughs viciously.

I excuse myself to the bathroom. When I'm back he's paid the check and standing up. He walks behind me up to the room. I love when he walks behind me.

I went shopping for tonight. I got myself new "lingerie" from H&M. It's 100% polyester and 150% flammable. It's a red romper with black polka dots and black lace trim. Not real lace, of course. Something sticky. If I wash this thing, it will melt.

"I like this look," he says, mocking me.

The bed is hard and squeaky and the room is decorated like an 80's beach house.

"It was super cheap."

"You're super cheap."

He tells me to sleep in the leash tonight, to make up for

"lost time." I've been a "bad slave" since I've forgotten to bring it around with me recently. He makes me carry it in my purse. As if my purse weren't heavy enough already. At first I was actually relieved when he gave me the leash—I thought that meant I was in control of when we would use it (ideally: never). "Have it with you every time you see me."

I thought he was joking. How stupid I am!

If he takes me out and I don't have it with me I'm in trouble—even if we're just having drinks or meeting for a quick coffee. Even if he just tells me to come outside of class so he can "say hi." He says making me do this is "kinky" but I think it's something else. I know the word for his behavior but I can't bring myself to say it. Once I admit to myself what he's doing, I'll have to admit what I'm allowing to be done.

A couple weeks ago he invited me to sleep over, out of the blue. His wife had a last-minute work trip or something. It was unexpected and I was unprepared. I came over right after school, at 21:30. The second I walked through the door he asked, "Where is it?"

I explained through tears that I had to carry extra stuff that day. "Piles of fabric and books and I'm always walking in heels and my knees hurt so much, and" – he cut me off. "I'm so disappointed. Go home."

When he starts snoring I consider removing it and putting it back on before he wakes up. But I decide that it's not worth the risk. I'll sleep when I'm dead, which may be sooner than later, if I'm not careful.

In the morning, I pretend to wake up shortly after he does. I open my eyes to find him watching me, proudly. His face is full of love as he unbuckles the belt. When the chain drops to the floor he says, "you're free."

Asshole.

17. HAPPY HOUSE

My boss has been insufferable ever since some loser left her. She thinks I've got bad taste but this woman exclusively dates shitheads. Of course she sleeps with models and rock stars but the men she ends up *with* are the worst. This one was secretly gay, the last one was secretly psychotic, the next one will be...secretly Santa?

Now the little free time she used to give me, when she'd go on romantic trips or have big arguments or whatever, well, that's gone. She calls me at all hours, coming up with reasons for me to work when there is no work to do.

"Mia, I found an error in your last mass email. Correct and re-send it." The two of us are squished in her office. She's bought more books. So many books. Not a good sign.

"But we've already sent three emails this week."

"So?"

We used to sit across from each other and now we sit next to each other. So she can see my screen. So I can't take any breaks.

"So, maybe we should take it easy on our contacts."

"Why would we do that?"

"Because people are asking to be taken off the mailing list."

Kind of hilarious.

"How many?" She's offended, as if it's my fault.

"About ten a week." It's more than ten but I don't have the heart to tell her.

"And what do you do when they ask you that?"

I pause. Am I supposed to lie here or tell her the truth? I go with the truth.

"I take them off."

"Are you crazy!?"

I should have lied.

"What am I supposed to do!?"

"Ignore them! Find everyone you took off the list and put them back on!"

"That would take hours."

"When you're done with that, fix the email and re-send it."

An alarm saves me. It's 13:00 and I head out to get our salads.

The mailing lists are just the start. All of a sudden all our flyers are ugly, all our DJs are shit, all our concepts are irrelevant. She's critical of herself and paranoid of others. Everyone is out to get her and anyone else throwing any kind of party—a rave in Berlin or a child's birthday in Venezuela—will sabotage the success of hers. I don't blame her. Often her fears come true. People really are against her.

She's easy to hate because she's a bitch. But she's only a "bitch" because she's a woman. I know it's cliché to say but it's only a cliché because it's so common, this problem. Anyone else doing anything important in Milan is a gay man or a straight man or a man who could go either way, he doesn't care as long as he is in control of whoever his dick is in. She's the only woman doing events of this scale in Milan. I wish I were exaggerating, but it's true. She is a force of nature. Sometimes I wish she could see herself the way I see her. Maybe then she'd relax...and give me a break.

When I asked for some nights off to study for exams, she

lost it.

I tried to explain but I should have known better. "If I don't improve they'll expel me. And my mom will kill me."

"Grow up, Mia! Don't mention your mother at work!"

"I wish I didn't have to. But I miss so much school for work. The 9-17:00 office hours are fine! It's the evenings I need free. I only bring up my mom because she pays 3k a year for this Uni."

"Well it is a shame that she's paying. You don't even care about fashion design. You should drop out. If you could go full-time with me I could promote you."

"I already *am* full-time."

I missed my winter exams completely. I'll have to do two years' worth of exams this summer. That won't be possible unless I make a big change.

"I'm sick of clubbing. I'm ready to go next-level," she says when I arrive with our lunch.

"You're joking," I say, setting down the plastic containers. "Who could be sick of clubbing? What's 'next-level' mean?"

She got a massive new contract. We've been working our way up to this, teaming up with dumb brands like Trussardi and Pucci. Nothing brands. This is huge. This is Dolce & GaFUCKINGbanna! It's like the biggest gig she's gotten, ever. She'll make loads of money and new contacts from it. She needs the next few weeks to go smooth and she needs me to be "with it."

"Who knows, one day you could do PR for them!"

"Who knows, one day I could clean their floors." I squirt oil onto the lettuce.

"Mia, if you don't take anything seriously nobody will take you seriously."

I can walk home from work in twenty minutes. The office is in Via Savona and I live in Via Borgazzi. It's a tiny street right by Corso Italia which is basically the center of the universe. My new place would be perfect if my new roommate weren't a sociopath hellbent on ruining my life.

The place has three bedrooms, a living room, a kitchen and a large(!) bathroom. It's on the fourth floor of a building that my boyfriend says is "too nice" for me.

When I brought him into my bedroom he gawked at the magazine pages and punk posters pinned to my walls. He seemed ashamed of me and said, "You're just a kid." Yeah, no shit. I thought you were into that.

My crazy roommate has the biggest room. The smallest room belongs to a girl from Genova. I haven't gotten to know her and don't plan to because all she does is wear capris and study law. As if Italy needs one more lawyer.

My room has a balcony with floor to ceiling windows but no blinds. I've taped fabric to the windows. Fabric I was supposed to use for a collection. It doesn't do much to keep the light out or to keep the construction workers building the apartment across the street from staring at me. But that doesn't bother me as much as the fact that my room has no door.

When I get home I always find my crazy roommate hanging out in my room. Wearing my clothes or reading my books or stealing my boys. One night I found her with Chris, a British model who's dear to me. I spend every minute with him when he comes here for work. I walked in on her giving him a stick-n-poke tattoo on his chest, in my bed. She said, "you've got better light in here!" Pointing to my blindless windows.

The old man who works the building, the doorman/manager/dickhead is a pain in my ass. He watches me come in and out and asks prying questions. "Where are you going dressed like that?" To hell, old man! Wanna join me?

He goes through my trash.

He came upstairs one day to teach me how to recycle

"properly." I guess I accidentally put some plastic in the paper bin or vice versa. *Colpa mia!* He acts as if you get a death penalty for doing it wrong. Lethal injection, please.

STANDA is the grocery store down the street. I like it because it's small. Too many food choices freak me out. Here I know exactly which aisles to cruise for my basics. I grab Tavernello, a bag of frozen peas, a box of frozen spinach, a pack of strawberry Activia and instant coffee. I used to buy Barilla spaghetti and tomato sauce for chewing and spitting but I don't do that anymore. It's a waste of money.

Every day a teen refugee stands outside asking for change. He could be a model. I give him what I can, just a few euros usually. I wonder if him and Max know each other. Max is a Nigerian dude who deals blow to Flow. Like the STANDA kid, he's young, hot and fresh off a boat. One night him and I were alone on the couch while Flow was passed out in her bed. He turned me on just by touching my legs, which never happens. I was overcome with passion. So I took him to Flow's bathroom.

We did it on the floor. I was so turned on I think I could have actually finished with him but he ruined it. When he took his pants off he had these strings tied around his waist that hung down his legs. He said they were religious. He was self-conscious about them the whole time we were doing it. And he couldn't look at me at all, he just stared at the bidet by my head. After he came he looked wretched. He left before his mess could spill out of me.

I don't take birth control anymore because when I did, I was reckless. I let anyone do me bareback as long as they promised to "pull out." They never did. Pregnancy doesn't scare me. Abortion is legal in Italy and I've taken so many Plan B pills they don't even make me sick anymore. Zina sent me a ten-pack of Plan B from Moscow after I complained to her that I spent all my cash on them at the pharmacy. She was horrified. "The men should pay for them!" Russians know chivalry.

What truly plagued me was the idea of having HIV. I stressed about it constantly. I planned how I'd break the news to my mother. When I finally got the nerve to get tested, convinced I was dying, prepped for the worst, the doctor looked at me and laughed. He said, "You're a white woman, don't worry." How dare he!

I said, "Listen, buddy, not only do I let countless dicks bust loads in me, I've shared heroin needles." He wasn't fazed. He asked, "Do you share these needles with black men or gay men?" I didn't know what to say. The answer to his question was "no" but I couldn't believe he had asked it! "I'm sure you're fine but I'll test you since you insist."

The doctor was Italian, of course. Racist prick. I didn't have anything, it turned out. That's when I did some Googling. The bruises I often found on my body were from aspirin. A tab dissolved in sparkling water is my morning routine! I decided to find a new hangover cure and begin budgeting for condoms. They sell them at STANDA.

After Max left, I laid on the floor for a minute. I decided I couldn't deal with what I'd just done in my own company. Even in a movie this would have been a "bad scene." A "rock bottom" moment. I woke Flow up in a panic. I was crying. Without missing a beat she told me not to worry. She had a "secret soap." It's a specialty in the Dominican Republic, all the women use it to "kill bacteria, babies and evil spirits!" When you're desperate you'll believe anything. Like an atheist praying in a crashing plane. I found the soap in her medicine cabinet. Funny I never noticed it all those mornings I'd rummage for toiletries. It's a pink bottle that looks like nail polish remover. It has an illustration of a carefree island girl on it. Tall and tan and young and lovely. I wished I were her. I sat on the bidet and used it all up. I sat there until I couldn't feel my legs.

18. MEGLIO STASERA CHE DOMANI

"I miss you," my boyfriend's voice crackles like a fireplace through my new Nokia. I still haven't told my mom that I lost my Blackberry. She'd never let me forget it.

"Well, who's fault is that?" I reply. He's so busy with his wholesome home life.

"What are you doing later?" he ignores my jab.

"Anything to stay out of my apartment." I can't believe how much I miss Maria. Her hurried typing, her incessant alarms, her clunky clothes and shoes thrown into corners. Her asking me passive-aggressively where I've been for three days and two nights. If only I'd known it was love. There's a hole in my chest where my resentment towards her used to be. I wonder who she's sharing our sacred space with now. Someone who has no idea how special it is. I'm a terrible friend. I don't deserve anything.

"Come to a party with me."

"Really? Tonight?" I guess his wife must be out of town.

"I'll pick you up in a taxi."

Lucky me. I'm wearing a navy-blue leopard print dress Zina sent me in the mail. I'm showered, shaved, moisturized, freshly hair-dyed and ready to rumble! When he texts, "outside" I bounce downstairs like a bunny.

He's in the front seat of the taxi...that's weird. I wave to him and walk around to the back.

Diocane.

Diomerda.

Dioporco!

The space in the back that divides his wife and me is no bigger than a Chihuahua. I say "ciao" under my breath and sit as far away from her as I can. My right hand is on the door and my left is a fist in my lap. I look her over stealthily. After two sightings, I can confirm that she owns no makeup. She's wearing basic blue jeans. Levi's 501's with a button fly. Her top is a repulsive turtleneck. Probably Prada. There's nothing radical about radical chic. She wears a bra with an underwire. Her legs are skinnier than mine. She smells like *Lola* by Marc Jacobs which I can't wear anymore. I'm gonna pass out.

She looks out the window and comments idiotically about everything we drive by. Oh, nice store. Wow, cool trees! And, "Great pizzeria! Mia, have you been?"

"Mia doesn't eat pizza."

He chimes in from the front seat. He's enjoying this. Sick sick sick.

"No way! That's crazy," she says out the window.

"Yeah. I *am* crazy."

I should carry a gun around for moments like this. Or enough pills to overdose.

Instead I'm carrying something more lethal. And he knows it's in my purse. He can hear the chains when the car turns. We all can. If I survive this I deserve an Oscar. If I survive this I deserve a new life. The wife keeps talking.

"Darling," she grabs his shoulder to get his attention. Or to piss me off. Either way, it's a hideous gesture. "Laura just had her baby! We must get her a gift."

"That's sad." I grumble under my breath.

"What, Mia?"

I clear my throat. "I said that's sad. I'm sad for women who have babies."

"What do you mean?" she asks, vapidly.

"I *mean* that when I walk by a homeless woman on the street and then a pregnant woman on the street, I think, "I'm so lucky that I'm not pregnant." Get it? Because I'd rather be homeless."

"Why would you say that?"

"Because when you have a baby your life is over. Duh."

"Maybe you need to grow up." she says.

Maybe you need to shut up.

I don't say that, but I should.

We pull into a gravel lot and I leap out of the car before it makes a full stop.

"Mia! What are you doing?" my boyfriend yells.

I look back at him, then his wife, then the door I left open. Sickos!

"See you inside!" I run in straight to the bar. I will drink myself into nothing. I'll burn this party to dust. The past the present and future are void. Every dimension is obliterated. It's over for everyone. Our last night on earth. I say, "Six shots of vodka!" and drink fast. No dinner, no shots of olive oil, no chance of survival. This place looks familiar. I laugh bitterly when I know. Here we are. The gallery where I met my scumbag married boyfriend in the first place. If I hadn't come that night my whole life would be different. No pictures of my butt in bookstores, no knowledge of what pee tastes like. No need to compete with a completely unremarkable woman.

My boss is here. She waves to me from a sofa. I nod back. My boyfriend and his wife walk in. They don't look happy. How could they be? He's in love with me! The wife goes to the bathroom and my boyfriend comes to the bar, next to me. I avoid his eyes, shoot my last three shots of vodka and tell the bartender, "My boyfriend's paying." Before he can say whatever rubbish he's thinking, I spin around and head for the door.

My boss grabs my arm. Wasn't she on the sofa like a second ago? Small women always sneak up on you!

"Mia, what's wrong?"

"Nothing."

"You're crying."

"Am I?" I touch my face and it's soaked. "Thanks for the info."

I brush her off, march outside sit on the gravel. I hug my knees and light a cigarette. I hear my boss yelling. I hear my name.

"Who do you think you are!?"

My boss has her back to the door. My boyfriend is standing in front of her. She must have stopped him on his way out to me. Sneaky small woman. I'm relieved. He looks down and says nothing. Like a kid being lectured by his mom. He makes eye contact with me through the glass. Is he sorry? It doesn't matter.

My boss yells, "You're pathetic."

I get up and walk into the night.

I wake up choking. I was sleeping with my mouth open like someone in an airplane. Now my head is full of sand. My throat is stuck together with Velcro. I close my mouth and swallow painfully. My eyes are swollen shut. I rub them to inspire circulation. My eyelids feel like puffy labias. I open one then the other. The only thing worse than an alcohol hangover is a crying (hysterically) hangover. My head throbs as I sit up. Nausea, dizziness and remorse. I'm fully clothed and covered in sweat. The sun blasts through my balcony. The construction workers across the street wave at me. I wave back.

My phone is in my hand. I've got a dozen missed calls

from Zina. Wait—what is it about Zina? There's something about Zina...something about Zina that I'm forgetting. I look around my room for clues. My luggage is in the middle of the floor, packed messily. It looks like an overstuffed beef sandwich from Arby's. Oh, right. Oh no. I missed my flight to Paris. I got so wasted I slept through my alarms, like Maria always does. This is a new low for me.

I send Zina texts full of lies and say I'll come another time. She calls me again and I decline. I go to the bathroom and look in the mirror. Haggard. Sad. Deflated. Chic? I look like a Hedi Slimane era YSL model who drowned. All hip bones and bloat. I sit on the toilet and try to pee but nothing comes out. My boyfriend once said it's insane that I don't pee every morning. We were getting ready for work in his bathroom. I told him drinking water is for pussies. He didn't laugh. He stopped laughing a while ago.

I scroll down to the most precious part of my phone. The texts between me and him. I caress the screen with my thumb, achingly. I inhale, hold my breath and hit *delete all*. Then I exhale, hold my breath and erase his number. "Good job, Mia." I say out loud. I flush for the sake of it.

I take a long "Croatian Shower." It's the kind of shower you take when you're too sick to stand and too lazy to fill up a bath. You sit in the dry tub, hold the shower handle over your head and water yourself like a plant. I study my single stomach roll and my razor bumps and find a hair on my nipple. I try to pull it out but I can't.

I wrap myself in a towel and go to the kitchen. I mix instant coffee powder in a pan of hot water. I pour myself a cup and sit at my desk. I open my laptop. I log into Facebook and go to his page. I hover over his profile picture with my mouse. I make a circle over his features. He never let me touch his face. I hover over our friendship settings. Then I block him.

"Almost done, you can do it!" I say out loud and feel embarrassed. I chug my coffee and burn my tongue.

I log into Skype and delete our conversations. Where do naked photos go when they're gone? Here comes the hard part. We've been emailing every day. At work, I'm not allowed to text but sending emails never raised suspicions. We have hundreds of them. Maybe thousands! I trash them all. Once they're in the trash folder I go in there, select them all again and I hit: DELETE FOREVER.

You can't kill me if I kill me first.

19. FINE DEL MONDO

What's worse: when you wake up crying? Or when you wake up fine, and then after a few moments you remember that you're not fine and then you start crying?

Suffering is wisdom. I understand all of the pain in the world. War, famine, natural disasters, a cancelled TV show... But this isn't the end of the world. That's the problem. Everything is still here. And just because I deleted his number doesn't mean he deleted mine.

He's calling me non-stop.

"What do you want from me? To be married?"

"No. I just don't want *you* to be married."

I hang up on him and he calls me again. I answer, sobbing.

He's like, "I hate myself when I hear you like this."

He knows nothing about hating himself.

I hang up again and turn my phone off.

My breakup playlist:

1. "Don't Speak" by No Doubt
2. "Let me go" by Joan Jett

3. "Parting Gift" by Fiona Apple
4. "What Katie Did" by The Libertines
5. "Modern Romance" by the Yeah Yeah Yeahs
6. "No Guilt" by The Waitresses
7. "Damaged Goods" by Gang of four
8. "Die on a Rope" by The Distillers
9. "Punk Rock Love" by The Casualties
10. "Wish Me Well (You Can Go to Hell)" by The Bouncing Souls

I wish I had a playlist of songs about women killing men. So far I only have:

"Poison Steak" by The Red Aunts. Maybe I should write some.

Can you break up with someone who was never your boyfriend? Absolutely. You can break up with anyone you want! My first breakup was with God, when I was seven.

I got over that faster than this.

Here's how you get over a break-up:

1. Dress up. When you've broken up with someone you know you will run into them eventually. You either hope for this or fear this. Either way, you must dress up for the occasion. You force yourself to wear good outfits every day, no matter where you're going or what you're doing. Just in case! Eventually, you get used to dressing up. You start wearing good outfits by default. You forget what you started dressing up for. After some time, this is the new you: you're a person who dresses well! Congratulations. You're a Sciura at Gattullo.
2. Find a hobby. Drinking counts.
3. Hate all men. Hating men is more effective if you

Tweet about hating men. *"Have you laughed at a man today? It's free!"*
4. Wait. Time heals all wounds! Wait until you feel better or wait until you die. Hope there is no afterlife because if there is, you will feel like crap there, too.
5. Rebuild your life! By destroying your life. When breaking up with your boyfriend, it's best to also break up with your boss and all of your friends.

"I'm sorry to tell you like this, over the phone, but I just can't take this workload anymore. I need to focus on school. This is my two-weeks-notice."

She hangs up on me and sends me hideous emails. Nonstop. They could make a novella - a radical feminist manifesto. A religious cult textbook! It's really, truly, scary stuff. "You always wanted to be the star and hog my attention!"... "You've stolen all of my friends and made them your own!" ... "You were using me and now you've abandoned me when I need you most!" ... "You are not welcome to any of my parties ever again!"

Well, that will help my next task: ditching all my friends. Now that I'm an unconnected nobody, it will happen naturally. I am anonymous, I am invisible, I am worthless. I can do whatever I want. I am free.

Milan is the most dangerous city in Europe. Let's prove it. I start going out alone, like I used to. But it's all different now. I was once fresh-faced and hopeful, trusting, willing, wanting something good for myself and everyone around me. Now I go out to feel miserable and share my misery with others. We are all scum.

I bum a cigarette from a chef on Viale Gian Galeazzo. I guess he's a chef because he's in the uniform. I take him into a basement. Every European apartment has a basement, it's not that creepy. We lie down on some bricks. When he gets on top of me I feel nothing and when he stands up I feel less. He buckles his belt and blabs about his wife. "I've never done something like this" and "it can't happen again." Guilty men are revolting. Chill dude, I don't care. I'm just trying to forget what my ex feels like.

One man down, a million to go.

My hair has grown long and my body is perfect. I'm wearing a gorgeous dress from Versace. It doesn't matter how I got it. I'm walking down Via Vigevano, laughing, with someone very attractive. It doesn't matter who he is.

I walk by Cape Town Café, one of our spots, and they are sitting outside together, the whole Banda. They're older than ever and look depressed. I stop when I see them and they grovel over me and ask me how I've been. I say, you know, something impressive. He can't take his eyes off me. I see regret wash over his face. I walk away like Naomi Campbell on the catwalk in the 90's. Her peak! He texts me. He texts me, or he calls me…hmmm…maybe he follows me? I haven't worked out the details yet. That's my fantasy at the moment. I have a few playing in rotation. I think of them as I walk around listening to music all day.

He knows what music I'm listening to in my headphones. I choose songs accordingly. He's inside my head and all around me. He sees the way I interact with baristas and the guy who sells me cigarettes. He's in my closet when I pick out my outfits. He watches me fall asleep. He doesn't watch me poop, that part I block out, for his sake.

I've always had The Man in my head, since I was a kid. I think all girls do. We perform for The Man. It's "the male gaze," I guess. But now The Man is HIM. And that makes things more complicated. Even when I'm home alone, being myself, I'm not alone or myself. He's there. And it sounds creepy but the alternative is no better. When I remind myself that he isn't actually there, that he doesn't actually watch me walk down the street and go through my iPod shuffle, that he doesn't congratulate me for eating salads or drinking water, that he never does see me or think about me, probably, everything loses meaning.

How do you say, "sorry for being a bitch" without saying "sorry" or admitting you're a bitch? I've finally apologized. To Maria. I was a cunt and she deserved better. She appreciated it. That's a relief, since she's my only friend now. Once a week we go bar hopping. She complains about work and looks around for men. I look around too, for him. Anytime I see someone with his build, his tasteless clothes, his bald head, I panic. I haven't run into him yet, but I keep hoping. It must happen sooner or later! I have to pass his place when I walk to and from school every day. Another genius perk of my problematic apartment.

One day I walk by his place on the way to class and see that guy I was supposed to shoot with in the parking lot. Yeah that gross little one. He's sitting at the coffee shop under the apartment. My ex and I used to get espressos here every morning before work. He'd always make me get a brioche I wouldn't eat. He'd rip cigarettes out of my mouth.

"Hey! What are you doing here?"

"Waiting for our man."

"Oh, where is he?"

"Upstairs. Getting a blowjob from a hooker."

"Oh, cool. Tell her I say hi."

"Who?"

"The hooker."

I walk away with my head down and watch my makeup soak into the sidewalk. I can't believe he's already got a new side girl. It's so easy for him. I've been screwing around too of course but not because I want to! I have no choice. You've gotta bang the ex's DNA out of your body. Women keep parts of the men we bone inside of us. It's true! We keep all of their trash and carry that weight with us while they walk around light as a feather.

The worst part about trying new guys is I've forgotten how to have normal sex. I need to re-train my brain. My reflexes are messed up from all that hardcore stuff he dragged me into. Now I flinch and jerk my head away anytime a guy lifts his hand. I shut my eyes and whimper, in preparation of being hit. An abused puppy.

The best way to get as many boys as possible in you in a short amount of time is with threesomes. Like a pig on a skewer. One night I picked up a gay couple who had never had a girl before. They explored me under posters of Madonna and Kylie Minogue. It was a highlight in my reel, for sure. Here are my rebounds so far: gay threesome, straight threesome, the guy who made me peg him, the guy who refused to leave my apartment (my psycho roommate's boyfriend had to kick him out), the guy who sells kebabs, the guy who was watching a football game and met me in the bathroom during halftime, the stalker who followed me home, the rose guy, the photographer, the other photographer, the third photographer, the DJ, the Sicilian gangster, the neighbor, the cop, the firefighter. It's been a couple months. I wrote a poem about how grim my new hookups are:

> SUL TRAM TORNO A CASA
> DOPO SERATA DA SCHIFO
> UN MOMENTO BRUTTO
> DI LUCIDITA'
> RICORDO IL TIPO...
> LA MIA FERMATA ARRIVATA.
> MI BUTTO PER STRADA

"Too fast to live too young to die" is a saying. I'm too dumb to live and too lazy to try. But now it's time to get healthy. I'm done with this lifestyle! Being vegetarian isn't enough, I'm going vegan. Just vegetables, water and crack. I'm kidding, I'm not going to do drugs for a while, they're too expensive now that nobody gives them to me for free anymore. Quitting drugs has always been easy. I don't get all the trouble other people have. Maybe my eating "disorder" saved me because I'm so good at refusing stuff I need for survival so refusing anything else is a piece of cake. Sure, I want to get high but I don't need it. Who really needs anything? My boys back home weren't so lucky. Jamie is in prison now, so is another ex of mine. The rest are in rehab or home with their parents. I don't call them anymore; I don't think they would like to talk to me. Maybe this breakup is what I get for leaving them all high-and dry. (Literally).

"It's crazy what you can accomplish while your boyfriend is in prison."

That being said, I'll never go sober. Sobriety is the worst eating disorder.

"Every day is a new opportunity to ruin a day completely for no reason."

When I get myself off now I have to watch porn so that my memories don't haunt me. No matter what fantasy I start out with in my head, my ex comes in out of nowhere, takes everything over, ruins the storyline and makes me cum and cry at the same time. So I watch the most twisted porn I can, to prevent the invasion.

I focus on my mental and physical *"chill"*. Health! Ever heard of it? Breakfast: bag of frozen peas. Lunch: bag of lettuce. Dinner: potato chips and whiskey. *"I will die alone but I'll die skinny."*

I have no friends except girls on the internet. I've found a new community on Tumblr. Girls who are sadder than me *"Anti-aging hack: die young."*

We revel in our desire to disappear, glamorously.

My bedroom has become a "safe space." A guy I brought over showed me that I have had blinds this whole time. Can you believe it? They're the old-fashioned wooden kinds, like my grandma in Sisak has. I didn't see the rope to pull them down, hiding on the side. I can finally shut the light *and* the construction workers out of my sight! But sometimes I don't. Because after all, I crave their company.

I even got someone to install a door *with a lock*, so my psycho roommate stays out. I'm not bothered by her anymore. She realized I'm already incapacitated by pain and that's no fun for a bully. There's only one thing I still need to do. Today is the day. No more excuses. I reach into my closet, on the top shelf, behind my sweaters. I feel it and shudder. I handle the leash like a poisonous snake, holding it at arm's reach away. I throw it into a plastic bag and tie the handles into a knot. I head to the elevator. Don't touch it, don't look at it, don't think about it. Once it's in the trash I breathe a sigh of relief. That night there's a knock on the door. It's our doorman. He is holding the bag.

"What is this?"

"Nothing."

"It doesn't go in the trash."

"Where does it go?"

"Not in the trash."

"Should I recycle it?"

"No!"

"What am I supposed to do?"

"Take it back."

"I don't want it! Therefore it's trash. Do you understand?"

"You can donate it, if you wish. There's a donation box down the street."

"Trust me, nobody wants this."

"Not my problem."

"What about my rights? I should be able to throw trash away in my own home!"

"This is not America! We dispose of things properly!"

He leaves the bag on the floor and walks out.

My ears are burning. My rage turns my stomach. This thing wants to haunt me and I will not let it. Damn you, old man. Only one person can make me feel shitty in this world and that person is me! I take back the power you had. I take back everything I gave you. I take back the time and the effort and the outfits and shaving my pussy and telling you jokes. I take back listening to your stupid stories about China and how many people think you're smart. You aren't even that smart. Just because you're bald and wear glasses.

I grab the bag and walk outside in my pajamas. I storm past Gattullo and STANDA and the tobacco bar and find the dirtiest trash can there is. I open the bag up and release the leash in the wild. I slam it, naked, among empty beer bottles, cigarette butts and bags of dog shit. No regrets.

20. THE BAUER

"Focus on a light in the distance and you won't get sick." It's like being hung-over in a tram, but glamorous. I'm on a party boat at the Venice Biennale. The Biennale is crazier than fashion week. More pretentious and seductive. This isn't the Biennale you can buy a ticket for. This isn't open to the public; it's not even open to locals! This is opening week, meant only for those who buy art, make art or inspire it. I'm talking exclusive parties with drunk celebrities, famous journalists, sleazy art dealers, prominent drug lords, royalty and... me. I'm nauseous from seasickness and dancing on top of the bar with a porn star. Everyone took pictures of us performing with each other. Kind of like the last scene in *Requiem for a Dream*, but without the dildos or paychecks. I'd throw myself overboard if I didn't have so much work to do.

I came here to assist Matt, a British artist I met through my ex-boss. (She was right, I stole her friends.) The three of us are staying in the same house. It's OK, she doesn't hate me anymore. I don't think anybody could hate who I am right now—the only feeling I inspire is pity. She let me come to the party she's hosting at the Bauer Hotel. She even painted my fingernails tonight. Hot pink, like my dress. I'm here to help

Matt set up for his show. This boat isn't his party or hers. This party could only belong to the Banda.

Why doesn't everyone talk about Venice constantly? How can this city be so close to Milan yet in a different galaxy? How is it allowed to exist? How is that fair? Sure, it smells like sewage and I can feel the ground shifting and sinking but that's pretty standard for me. I've gotten lost every day. I go out to buy cigarettes and end up in a dingy dead-end alley full of ghosts. Before my life turns into a horror film a pigeon swoops in and leads me to San Marco Square. This week I've spent a thousand years sitting in the lobby of the Bauer Hotel. Everyone comes through there. I've met Marina Abramovic (she's a bummer), Courtney Love (she's a genius), Elton John (he's a bore) and Jeff Koons (I've hated him ever since he broke Cicciolina's heart).

Before I stripped for hundreds of people, I was feeling cool and composed. I made the rounds, met random try-hards and got some drinks at the bar. Standard. Then the wife came and stood next to me. Why the hell did she do that? She could have stood anywhere! She tried to make small talk so I did what any normal person would do. I ran away to the storage room. My plan was to hide but my ex was in there, looking for a bottle. He said he liked my dress and slapped me in the face. Then he pushed me outside and onto the bar and told me to dance, "bitch."

I'm stuck in a nightmare. You can't get off a party boat until it docks. My ex looks so good tonight that I feel personally insulted by it. He's wearing a white suit. The Banda are all dressed up too, like gangsters. It's a twisted family reunion. They know me better than anyone and they know all of my worst parts.

After my performance the photographer helps me vomit into the trash with his hand down my throat. He says I'm shivering and I take his word for it. He gives me a sweater. "We love our Pupa" he tells me. I know.

We finally dock. Matt is waiting for me outside, to take me to another party.

"How was it?"

"A mess."

"Why?"

"He slapped me."

"Who?"

"My ex." I point to the blinding white suit.

"He slapped you? Are you serious?"

"He's not allowed to do that anymore."

Matt isn't listening, he's over there now, threatening to throw him in the canal. It's so embarrassing when people stand up for me. They don't understand that it isn't worth it. And that this is all my fault.

One day I woke up miraculously lucid. A ridiculous idea struck me.

"Don't make fun of me but…I think I want to…look at the art today?" I told Matt over breakfast.

"Mia. You realize I'm an artist, right?"

I stared at him blankly while chewing my cereal.

"So why would I make fun of you?" he continued.

"Exactly for that reason."

Matt gave me his pass. I support the arts but do the arts support me? I've never enjoyed museums or galleries because they make me feel useless. And bored. But I thought, "let's be cultured!" Well, guess who else is cultured? My ex and his wife. Seeing them hold hands in the Polish pavilion hurt more than watching Paris Hilton die in *House of Wax*. To make matters worse, I was alone, hung-over and wearing…flip-flops.

They didn't see me. I hid behind a sculpture.

Let me explain the footwear. My shoes broke and I'm broke as well. The one pair of sandals I brought to Venice fell apart from dragging myself on the gallery floor on my hands and knees. Matt needed me to glue millions of tiny squares onto an endless piece of fabric for his show. Now I can't afford a new pair, not even at H&M.

Matt didn't pay for my work in money. My fee was: train tickets, the bed in the house (which we shared), water taxis and salads, which he force-fed me. The parties are all open bar once you find your way into them. Anyway, I had to buy flip-flops from a street vendor. Truly my darkest moment. Put it on my gravestone. Hopefully soon.

The Biennale ended last week. Matt and my boss left me alone with the keys. For days nobody checked on me. I threw never-ending parties for foreign journalists I met at the Bauer or through Matt or in some alley previously. Their flights are long so they hung around longer than they should. People who don't want to go home, like me. I've been seeing an editor of a fashion magazine. He gave me loads of funny pills I've never tried before. He's from Korea. "North or South?" I asked as a joke. He didn't think it was funny. I wonder if he knows Handley.

We had a bedroom, but he only wanted to have sex outside. Between the recycling bins, next to a fountain, behind a bench, against a boat. In the hallway. On a neighbor's door. They must have complained. The lady who gave Matt the house freaked out when she heard I was still there. So I kicked my foreign press out and spent a day cleaning up. Bags of trash, myself included. When I handed the landlady her keys I realized I have nowhere to sleep. And I'm not going back to Milan in flip-flops.

I walk to the Bauer. I know my way around town now. And I know which lobby chair I can sleep in. I curl up on the leather like a cat and hope nobody notices. As I start to drift off someone taps me on the shoulder. It's probably a cop. The Bauer staff finally had enough of me. That's fine. I'll do well in prison. I don't mind dating girls. I can sleep on any hard surface. I'm not affected by bad or irregular meals in any way. And being bossed around is second nature to me. I open my eyes, ready to be taken to my new life. Oh. It's just that art dealer I met through Matt.

"Mia, right?"

"Yeah. And you're…Travis?"

"John."

"Sorry. I'm always too drunk to remember names."

The truth is I have an excellent memory, trashed or not. I can recall what I wore one day fifteen years ago. My brain just naturally trashes most names because I come across so many. Who knew I'd ever need this dude? He's over fifty and out of his mind! He has gold teeth and spiky grey hair, like a flamboyant pirate. He dresses pretty well though, all Alexander McQueen.

"What are you doing here?"

"Making this chair my new bed."

"What do you mean?"

"I mean now you can say you're friends with a homeless person."

He laughs and says, "come on." Everyone thinks I'm joking when I'm not and doesn't think I'm joking when I am.

He takes me to the bar. I haven't had a drink here yet—I've been sitting around for free all this time. Every cocktail at the Bauer is thirty euros. When he's drunk he asks for my number so we can "hang out" sometime. I say, "why wait? I'll give you my number *and* let you take me to your room. Now." I'm tired and I know what I've still got to do before I can go to sleep. His room isn't as big as I thought it would be. But his dick is monstrous. He's like, "Why didn't we get together last week?" And I'm like, "Because last week I had a home."

In the morning, I take a shower. The bathroom has gold lighting and cold tiles. There's a stack of fluffy towels and piles of artisanal soaps and lotions. I stuff some into my purse. There's a pair of women's shoes under the sink. They're Top

Shop wooden clogs with black leather straps. Size 40. I guess the last girl he banged made a run for it the minute she saw his dong. Some just can't handle it. The shoes are just my size. I put them on and leave my flip-flops in their place. Now I can go to Milan. I grab a pack of cigarettes from his desk on my way out.

When I get on the boat to the train station he texts me.

"You stole from me!"

"I needed new shoes. Those…aren't yours, are they?"

"What shoes? I mean the cigarettes."

"Oh, do you mind?" He has a room at the Bauer for Christ's sake! I didn't think he'd notice the cigarettes.

"Yes I mind! The cigarette box is filled with hash!"

I hate hash. I give the pack of cigarettes to a tourist. On the train, Flow calls to say that she's "worried" because my ass is on the cover page of Dagospia magazine. But I know that "worried" is just another word for "jealous."

21. ALMENO LA MORTE È GRATIS

Have you studied the French Revolution? I haven't, but I've watched all of Sophia Coppola's films. And this summer I guillotined my old self like Marie Antoinette (starring Kirsten Dunst).

Every revolution is inspired by suffering. Things had to get dark first. I used every cell in my body to force my brain to tell myself to "get my shit together." I mean study. I only managed, I only survived, physically—because I didn't study at home. I studied at bars, cafés, on park benches and McDonald's. This way I felt like I was "part of the world" while being cast out of it.

Effort is embarrassing. Nothing to be proud of! I did it though. I passed my exams and I only had to cheat on a few of them. Theory, costume history and textile arts are easy bluffs. The real challenge was sewing my collection after skipping every single sewing class. I figured, most fashion is "Made in China" these days anyway. So it would be practical of me, professional, even, to outsource the work. I went to Paolo Sarpi, Milan's so-called "Chinatown," though it's more of a "Chinastreet." It took all day and a few bubble teas but I found a seamstress for cheap. Pretty genius, if you ask me.

My mom rewarded my passing grades with a plane ticket home. She probably knew I'd spiral without it. Have you ever spent August in Milan? That's some *Girl, Interrupted* shit. No looney bin for me (this time)! I got to spend my summer in civilization. I went to: WALGREENS, CVS PHARMACY, 7/11, WAL-MART, K-MART and THE MALL. I experienced AIR-CONDITIONING and 24/7 GROCERIES and HUGE CEMENT SIDEWALKS and WATER WITH ICE IN IT! I drowned myself in STARBUCKS. Even my sweat is jacked up. I got to drive my car on the highway. I got to speak English. I forgot how funny I am in English! I'm the goddamn Joker. There wasn't a dry seat left at WAFFLE HOUSE.

Jamie called me up one day. He was like, "I got out of prison!"

"Congratulations!" I cheered. "I got out of Milan!"

"Wanna celebrate?"

"I never don't."

We met in a parking lot by the university. He looked shrunken. He wore the same outfit I met him in years ago but it fit differently. Ratty black jeans, a studded belt, that Cramps shirt hanging on by a thread. He dyed half of his hair blonde and the other blood red. He smelled like Old Spice when I hugged him. Part of me hoped he had heroin in his pocket but most of me hoped that he didn't. I was like a groom with cold feet expecting his bride to arrive at the altar but secretly wishing she runs. She did.

"I get these from the doctor." He held out a flat orange pill. It's called Suboxone. It's the state-approved heroin replacement for junkies. "This shit is wild," he said.

I didn't believe him. He only let me take a tiny piece. You don't swallow it like a regular pill or smash it up and snort it or melt it and shoot it up. You dissolve it under your tongue. It tastes the way TV static looks. And when you vomit from the vertigo what comes out looks like orange slushie. He drove me back to his mom's house. I used to wait all week just to go there. I used to wish I could live there. This time the image depressed me. When he pulled up, I couldn't believe how pitiful it was. I imagined a wrecking ball slamming into it.

We had sloppy sex and he rolled over and cried afterwards.

I don't think he was crying about me.

I went blonde. It took weeks of processing since I had ten-years-worth of black hair dye in there. It took three sessions of combined twelve hours to get down to my natural color (wet mouse) and another three sessions of combined twelve hours to lift that to *Barbie*. Now you know: when you watch an action movie starring Angelina Jolie or Megan Fox or Jessica Alba and a she goes to a public restroom to change her image completely using just a new shade of lipstick and boxed hair dye—if she goes blonde, you know that scene is less realistic than the aliens chasing her.

My friend said what she did for me is worth $1,200 in salon visits but she didn't make me pay because she's still a student. Also, she's "owed me" big since high school. I initiated her into the punk scene, introduced her to her nasty boyfriend and acted as an alibi when she skipped school. I'm probably part of the reason she's in beauty school and not regular college right now. Anyway, I've always said it's better to be cool than pretty but now that I look pretty I realize I've been full of shit my whole life.

I used to hate dumb blondes in school and now I am a dumb blonde and that is growth. It's a pain in the butt, I'll admit. *"Blondes don't have more fun but they do have a higher pain tolerance."* That Tweet got a hundred likes.

My mom got me a summer pass to her gym. We went every morning before she'd go to work. She ran laps on the track upstairs and I played with the machines. It was unpleasant, but I guess there are worse things that can happen to me than physical activity. The treadmills are by the TV so they're just an excuse to watch *The View*. The weight room has no TV. So in there I'd listen to music and fantasize about returning to Milan as a "better me." After the gym, we'd go to Foster's Market for scones and coffee. She used to take me there in high school. I'd always say, "I'm gonna eat my scone in class," but I'd give it away. Random boys I'd see in the hallway mistook my illness for a crush. This summer I ate the pastries. I don't see any difference in my body, but working out helps me not want to murder myself when I eat. If I consider how much time I've spent counting calories or obsessing about food I realize I could have done a lot of other stuff in that time. I just don't know what, exactly.

My mom bought me a new wardrobe from American Apparel. There's no American Apparel store where I'm from. She looked over my shoulder as I put stuff in an online shopping cart. "Are you sure? It's like, $50." I'd say with each click, flooded by endorphins. She said she felt bad sending me back to a country "full of well-dressed assholes." I'm the asshole. When I thought about how much she loves me and how much I lie to her I considered hanging myself with the mesh bodysuit I added to the cart. But that would be a waste of mesh.

"Let's not cry," she said at the airport.

"Ok," I said, bursting into tears.

"You have all of your stuff, right? Passport, money, laptop?"

"Yeah." I said, sobbing uncontrollably.

"It's just school!"

She hugged me. "You'll be home soon."

If only either of those were true. I kissed her and went through security. I was in such a hurry to get to a point where I couldn't see her if I turned around, that I left my carry-on bag on the carousel. The security chased me down and made a big fuss about it. They were like, "Your bag could have been a bomb." I wish. So I wrote REMEMBER CARRY-ON on my hand with a Sharpie. Later, on the airplane, the man sitting next to me said, "I think that's so inspiring."

"What?" I said.

"The message on your hand."

I looked at my palms, in confusion.

"Remember, carry on," he said, and closed his eyes.

I land in Milan in the morning. I take a bus from Malpensa to Centrale and take a tram from Centrale to Bocconi and walk from there to my apartment. When I arrive it's the afternoon. My roommates aren't there but two boys are.

"Ciao." I say, throwing my luggage down in the hallway.

"Ciao," they answer. They're in the kitchen. The good looking one is sitting at the table, in a bathrobe and slippers, smoking a cigarette. The regular looking one is standing by the stove making Italian coffee. He's wearing khakis and a button-up shirt.

"I'm…Mia. I live in there." I point to my bedroom.

"Yeah we know. I'm _____ and that's _____." The regular looking one says.

I don't hear their names because I'm not paying attention.

"Are you friends of my roommates?"

"No, *we* are your roommates." The good looking one says.

"What?"

"They didn't tell you?"

The coffee boils over the Moka pot. The regular looking one turns off the stove.

"No. We don't talk anymore," I say. "Can I have some?"

"Sorry, there isn't enough for all three of us," the regular looking one says, pouring himself a cup. He also pours the good looking one a cup. Then he turns the Moka upside-down in the sink and says, "You see? Now it's empty."

"You can have mine," the good looking one says. I take his

cup and sip the grainy, burnt coffee. Disgusting, I wish I hadn't asked. Now I have to finish it because it was a gift. "Mmm, *grazie*," I say, smiling.

The regular looking one enjoys his coffee while explaining the situation. Last month the psycho roommate had to move back to her hometown for undisclosed reasons. I'm guessing she was institutionalized. The other, less psycho (but very annoying) one took that as an opportunity to move out as well. Now she lives with her law professor, near Castello. She told the boys that she's engaged to be married to him (what an idiot).

So I live with these two dudes now. They're Bocconi students. The regular looking one is from Sardegna and the good looking one is from Bari. I've never heard of Bari.

"How did those girls find you guys? You don't seem like anyone they'd know." Or anyone I would know.

"The internet. Ever heard of it?" The good looking one winks at me.

I'm the luckiest girl in the world.

The good looking one looks like James Franco but with bright blue eyes and no wrinkles. I get in the bath and masturbate about him. When I finish I decide I won't do that again. And I definitely won't ever sleep with him. Then again, it's silly to make any promises this early in the school year. I mean, it's only my first day back.

I sit on my bed wrapped in my towel and consider unpacking my luggage. But it's a beautiful day. I decide to get dressed and go out.

The streets are full of horny hope. The Milanesi are back from *vacanza*. Everyone's boat-sick and willing to stick their dick in a pretty blonde. I don't have anything particular to do but I'm optimistic. I'm wearing a dress I made—I mean, had that lady in Chinatown make—for my exams. It's baby pink silk with black lace on top. Asymmetrical, one shoulder out. The cut showcases my collarbones and neck, which hasn't been choked in months. Tonight I'll try to meet up with Maria or check out some parties.

For now, I'm savoring a solo aperitivo. Negroni and potato chips on a wobbly table in Ticinese. I smile at people walking by. I probably look suspicious. Is this what it feels like to be a moron—I mean, a normal person?

"Hey baby, are you in town?"

Just because I deleted his phone number from my contacts doesn't mean I don't recognize the phone number itself. I must have memorized it by accident. And by that, I mean on purpose. My heart drops into my bowels. "It's just a text." I say out loud. A lady at another table looks at me funny. "Calm down," I tell myself. I take the phone into my shaking hands and type.

"Landed today."

"Can we meet at PRAVDA? I need to talk to you. It's important."

Oh, my god, it's happening. Why did it take so long? Maybe he wanted me to resolve my issues. I finally studied, started eating, went blonde—how does he know? He must be spying on my Facebook. He made a new, fake profile so that he could check on me every day. I knew today was a good day but I didn't realize it was *the day* I've had dreams about. I'd wake up furious that they were just dreams.

I leave money on the table and stand up so fast I knock the glass over. "Sorry!" I exclaim. The lady at the other table makes a face at me. "Che cazzo voi?" I say, dashing away rabidly. I don't care what that Sciura thinks. She can't imagine the scope of what's just happened!

The PRAVDA bartender makes my signature gimlet before I can order it. I don't tell him that's not my drink anymore. You can't tell a bartender that what they've been careful and kind enough to remember about you is now irrelevant. Only a prick would do that. The gimlet is not strong enough for this. I order a second one before I finish it.

Seeing him walk in is punch in the pussy. But I'm not nervous. Being with him is natural, like taking a piss between two parked cars outside of Plastic.

"Hi Blondie." He leans in and kisses me on the cheek like a polite Italian. "What are you wearing?"

"I made it! You like it?"

"I don't like asymmetrical things."

Just then the photographer walks in. Why is he here? That guy gets on my nerves. He never even introduced me to Pete Doherty. My ex and the photographer hug a little too long. Something doesn't feel right. This isn't like it was in my dream.

"So, guys," my ex looks at me the way he did that night after Paris. He's nervous.

"I wanted to bring you here, and tell you in person, because you're family,"

"We're your Banda, baby!" The photographer says, patting my ex on the back.

I don't say anything. I don't like this.

My ex looks at me, then looks down and says to his feet, "My wife and I are having a baby."

He looks back up at me and I don't know what he sees. Probably something similar to a painting I had to study this summer. The one called "The Scream."

"Congrats!" The photographer hugs him. "Do you know when it happened?"

"In Venice...something was in the air."

I can't breathe. I'm a rat sinking with the Titanic.

"Can I have another drink?" my voice cracks.

"Mia, you can be the babysitter!" The photographer grins at me like Devil in the *Powerpuff Girls*. His eyes shine with glee. He knows what he just did to me and he likes it. Sadico di merda. Is this why my ex brought him here? To make fun of me? I won't let him win. I'm gonna be cool.

"Good idea." I say, grabbing my cocktail, "but I'm bad with kids." I try to take a sip, but my body betrays me. My eyes well up. A tear plops into the gimlet. He'd enjoy it if I cried. I cover my face with one hand and run outside. On the sidewalk I can't see and I can't move. I collapse on the street.

All the work I've done on myself is erased. I'm the same crummy person, with a makeover. I put my head between my knees and see the photographer's shoes in front of me. Now they're circling. He didn't come out to apologize or try to console me. He's got a camera in his hands. He's filming me while I weep. I don't have the strength to tell him to stop. It doesn't matter. I don't matter. Eventually my ex comes outside and throws me into a cab that he called. He tells the driver my address and hands him cash because I can't move or speak.

The next day the photographer posts a video on Vimeo. Titled, "Love Is A Pain In The Ass." Me crying on the street for five minutes, cut off when my ex walks into frame. Fashion school girls will do just about anything to have an acclaimed photographer make a film of one of their dresses, am I right?

Have you not seen my editorials? "Of course."
"Does it bother you to be touched by men?"
"Nothing bothers me."
"You start this weekend."
He shook my sweaty hand.

The club has a few rules. One, no sex in the private rooms.
Two, don't lock the bathroom. All the girls have one bathroom we share, which is out in the entrance hall. Management took the lock off the door to keep us from "doing drugs"
in there. It's really rude, because now we've gotta use one
hand to keep the door shut while using the other to do drugs.
The last rule is don't sit with clients unless they buy you
drinks. We don't make tips for dancing like American strippers. Nobody throws cash on stage. I guess it's because euro
singles come in coin form...throwing them at us would leave
bruises. We dance for free and make money only from selling
drinks and lap dances. I don't sell much of either. My stage
name is Elle Lay. I don't have any STDs but my persona does.

The club is called LAP ZEPPELIN (brilliant) near Loreto
(brutal), pretty far from me. By the time I'm off work I
collapse. I don't go to parties anymore. Nights I come home
from school, get drunk with Filip and go to work. Filip is my
new best friend. I think he may be my soul mate. I've never
met anyone like him. A while ago he wrote me on Facebook,
out of the blue. He said he saw me on Vimeo and thought, *we
should be best friends*. I figured, anyone who saw *that* and
wanted to be friends with me...might be onto something.

We met that night at McDonald's. He was dressed in a grey
Zara suit. I saw it in the store a week ago. He didn't have any
socks on so his ankles popped out of his cherry Dr. Martens
shoes. I've seen him around school but never inside a class-
room. I remember watching him eat ice cream in the cafeteria
and thinking he was hot. He's tall and thin, with an ancient

bone structure and bushy eyebrows like my grandfather had. If he weren't gay I'd fall in love. We fell in love in another way. We clicked instantly. My Slavic brother!

"Two shots of vodka, please," he ordered. We began the night at a crappy bar in 24 Maggio. A place construction workers and delivery boys stop in for grappa to keep warm. When the shots arrived, he took both. Then he looked at me and said, "What will you have?"

"You drink even more than I do," I said.

"I drink more than anyone. Even me!" he said and laughed, tilting his head back.

He's Polish but he grew up in Tuscany so we've got basic stuff in common. Like: feeling out of place no matter where we go and knowing that deep down we're just hoes. He's crazier than me. He has funnier stories. He *is* funnier.

"Wanna go to a fashion party with me?" I asked. It was already September, known to our kind as "fashion month."

"Only if we aren't on the list!" he said.

I was on the list, but for kicks we snuck in through a back door. The party was for Fendi. They held it in a warehouse in the south of town. Open bar, open legs, open minds! I wasn't on any stimulants but I felt a surge of serotonin whenever I'd look over and see Filip next to me. He made me not miss my ex. He made me not miss anything. For the first time in forever I felt a wormhole open up in front of me. I could finally leap forward.

We woke up in someone's bathtub, covered in confetti. We walked home, about two kilometers. McDonald's for breakfast. We sat there talking for hours. We pieced things together and realized we're both in that porn magazine. That one I (supposedly) did for Pete Doherty. He was on the front cover. Well, his cum was, splashed onto an Adidas slipper. His story comes right after my centerfold. If that's not a sign then what is? He walked me home.

"That was fun," I said.

"Yeah. What are you doing tomorrow?"

"Nothing, you?"

"I'll pick you up in the morning. I live just over there," he pointed across the street, past Gattullo.

Since then we've been together every day. We've drunk countless boxes of Tavernello. We've been kicked out of every club. So we don't go to clubs anymore. We tried to see Peaches live but were so wasted we fell asleep on the bus on the way there and missed the show. He helped buy my first stripper shoes. He was a teenage stripper in Warsaw. He inspired me to start stripping. He inspires me to do everything.

He's inspiring!

The shoes are black Gothic Lolita Pleasers. I bring my work shoes and work clothes to work in that ugly purse I still have. This purse could survive the apocalypse. It already has survived my personal apocalypse, after all. I'm not the prettiest stripper by any means but I am the most stylish. I get my outfits in Paolo Sarpi. Sometimes I'm a nurse, sometimes I'm a cat, sometimes I'm a schoolgirl. But usually I'm just myself.

A scrappy party girl who doesn't party anymore.

I've got a good routine now. Every morning Filip picks me up. We have coffee together at California Bakery and then we walk together to NABA . I don't look at my ex's house when we pass it. During his daytime classes I hang out at NABAR. I spend my time on Tumblr and wait for Filip to come out for cigarette breaks. During my night classes, he hangs out at NABAR and waits around for me to do the same. Sometimes we both skip our classes and spend the whole day watching *Strangers with Candy* on our laptops. When we're both done with school we walk home together. Filip lives a few blocks away from me, in a gated area we call "KOSOVO." We call it that because it looks like Kosovo. Before we actually go home we hang out in our favorite bar: Col Di Lana #1. Whiskey costs three euros per glass. We call whiskey liquid gold. We drink as much as we can until we can't stand.

"Would you rather be skinny, happy or successful?" I ask.

"I'd rather be dead."

Everyone at school knows about my job because I channel it in my new projects.

This year's collection is called:

STRIPPERS FROM OUTER SPACE.

I present my work:

"All my life I was sad that I couldn't go into outer space. Like, for years, it kept me up at night! It was so unfair, I thought. And then one night, I was really high, and I realized, bitch, you ARE in outer space! You were BORN in outer space! Planet Earth is the VIP room of outer space! Right? So I was happy about that but I was still sad about the fact that I couldn't time travel. Right? But then another night I got really, *really* high and I realized...like, I AM time traveling right now!!! We are all time traveling, that's literally what "getting old" is. So anyway, this collection is about living your fantasies all of the time. Sometimes you live out your fantasy on purpose and sometimes by mistake. Usually by mistake."

My classmates are all *"perbene"* Italians. They don't get it.

"How can you take your clothes off for money?"

"I don't know...maybe because I'm hotter than you?"

"All strippers are comedians but not all comedians are strippers." I Tweet through their boring presentations. They're just jealous that I'm a genius.

My whole life I thought that being nice was a good thing.

Filip taught me otherwise. Being nice isn't nice at all. Being nice is the reason why people have been so mean to me. Being nice makes people uncomfortable because it makes them feel pressured to be nice in return. But they don't know how or aren't willing to do that. So you being nice makes them feel bad. And when they feel bad they treat you badly.

I'm trying to practice being mean because that's what people like. That's why I'm excelling at Lap Zeppelin. I have yet to decide who's more annoying: my classmates or my clients.

"You don't belong here."

All of my clients say that. They think they're so original.

"Why do you say that?"

"You're too smart to be a stripper."

All of my clients say that. They're so dumb.

"Nobody is too smart to be a stripper. Only too stupid to consider doing it. I can pay my rent with what I make *tonight*. Can you do that?"

"Do what? Pay my rent tonight?"

"No. Can you pay MY rent?"

Filip doesn't let anyone push him around. He does all the pushing. When he's on a date with a guy who treats him badly, bores him, or says the wrong thing, Filip will point in some direction and say, "Look over there!" And when they look over there, Filip will run into the Metro and disappear forever.

Everything inside the strip club is leopard print and velvet lit with neon. There's just one stage with two poles, a tiny bar with a bitter bartender who was a stripper ages ago. Our dressing room is even smaller than the bar. We don't have lockers or chairs or mirrors with lights on them, like you see in all the Tumblr pictures of #strippers. We have two benches facing each other and we all have to fit on them. Our personal items go in plastic boxes under the benches. When we change or clean ourselves with baby wipes or rest or chat, we sit thigh-to-thigh.

The girls are from Romania and Nigeria and Southern Italy. I'm the only Croatian or American. Russians and Northern Italians strip at the chicer clubs, near the Duomo. I first applied to work at Foca Loca. They laughed in my face and sent me to a crummier place, which sent me to a crummier place, which sent me to a crummier place, which sent me to Lap Zeppelin. I'm really glad these guys hired me because the next step would be in Bovisa.

All the girls are nice to me. It's like *Sisterhood of the Traveling Thongs*. Maybe because I'm a bad dancer and that's fun for them to watch. My hands are always sweaty and I make the poles too wet to even try pole tricks. I mostly just throw myself around on the floor and mimic moves I've seen in Britney Spears music videos. The DJ plays Gaga when I'm on stage, which is good branding on his part. I get it. I'm the "weird pale girl." But I've begged him to stop, because her songs trigger bad memories. Nobody wants a sad girl on stage. Or maybe they do. Anyway, he didn't listen. He doesn't care. He's pretty terrible. Whenever the Nigerian girls get on sage he says, "Smile, girls! Show your teeth, or we can't see you!"

He says the same racist jokes every night.

I like watching the other girls dance. They're professional. They know what they are and aren't supposed to do. So do I, but I don't listen. I keep giving my number to clients.

Now I have numbers saved in my phone as:

"No"

"No2"

"No3"

"definitely NO!"

"NO NO NO NO"

"NO DO NOT ANSWER!"

"CERTIFIED SERIAL KILLER"

I've been on dates with clients too. A Bulgarian drove me home after a shift. We had a morning date at a vending machine near my place. The next day he took me out to lunch, but it didn't go well. He loves the brand GUESS and the waitress was in head-to-toe GUESS and they fell in love over it. I purposefully spent a long time in the bathroom so he could ask for her number.

I met a hot young lawyer at the club. He got a bottle for me and bought three dances. The next night he took me to dinner and walked me to work. I went down on him in a park. That weekend he asked me out for drinks and I kind of ruined it because I brought Filip with me. In retrospect that was a bad move. Filip and I are generally Slavic Brutalism but after a drink we become Art Deco. After two drinks we're Dada. A urinal in your face! I'll take Filip over a lawyer any day.

My "regulars" are hilarious. One of them pays to just talk dirty to me. Another is a tired taxi driver who takes naps on my lap. I have a Chinese client who gets really sassy when I don't touch his dick. One night he tried to rape me and security threw him out. They were so scandalized, they kept apologizing because it took them so long to "save me." I tried to explain that it wasn't a big deal.

The thing about rape is that it isn't always the worst thing that happens to a woman. Sometimes it's not even the worst thing that happens to us that day.

On my way home from the club Filip calls me. He's screaming for help.

"She's chasing me down the street!"

"Filip! Who's chasing you?"

"The woman from the tram!"

Oh, *that* woman. I know her. She's a walking corpse. Anna Dello Russo gone rotten. Once I found myself alone on a tram with her and she cursed me. Something that will be passed onto my kids. But I won't have any. I don't want to give my bad omens or bad genes to anyone. Hangovers run in my family.

"Run towards me and I'll run towards you." I say.

I know the direction he's coming from. The tram stop by Bocconi. I start running in my stripper shoes. I see him coming towards me, screaming.

"Keep running, Filip! RUN!"

We reach each other and embrace. She flies towards us. We hold hands and sprint to my place. In the elevator we're safe. My post-work tradition is making a bowl of soup and watching cartoons. They sell them at STANDA: for a euro you can have a bag of creamed broccoli, potato, minestrone or farro soup that comes in a powder. You just pour it in boiling water. I eat it while watching *Sealab 2021*. I usually only get through one episode. This job makes me sleep like a baby.

I make Filip my last bag of soup and he passes out on the couch.

The next morning over coffee my good looking roommate says, "can you try to bring *more* freaks into this house?"

I tell him, "only if you try to leave *more* piss on the toilet seat."

He says, "vaffanculo" and storms into his bedroom.

"Grazie amore!" I yell at him.

He slams his door and I head to the bath. His temper is inspiring.

23. CHICKEN PARISIAN

I'm a bad person but a good animal. My body isn't broken after all. (At least not in this way.) I had my first *shared* orgasm...with a client. Ten minutes later, I had my second. Third, fourth, hundredth. It happens all the time, at work. If I'd known "exotic dancing" was my secret I would have started at sixteen! *"Everything is about sex except for sex. Sex is about memes."* I Tweet between dances.

I'm so inspired! Maybe it's my outfits. Or the controlled circumstances. It's the money. Or the body guards waiting for me. It's a scent they put in the air. Perhaps watching the girls dance all night keeps me turned on. Either way, this is my secret. I don't just play along anymore and I don't fake with anyone. I'm a real part of it. A part of the world! Sex used to make me feel drained. Now I'm exhilarated. Every time I finish with a guy he loses something I gain. Golden chips, magic mushrooms and shooting stars. Since *actual* sex is forbidden in the private rooms I do what I can. The first three bases. Sports!

Tonight I got a client in a wheelchair. He asked me to stand over him.

"You're really good at this." I say, checking my butt in the triple mirrors.

"You're surprised because I'm in a wheelchair?"

"No, I'm surprised because you're a man."

I can't believe I'm getting paid to have a personal revolution. I'm their best girl! I still can't dance but I've got special powers. And people are catching on.

The manager asks to see me in her office.

She's a deeply wrinkled woman with a deeply disturbing fashion sense.

"We need to talk," she says, lighting a cigarette.

We aren't supposed to smoke in here. But we all do.

"Am I in trouble?" I ask, taking a smoke from her pack.

"Mia, you're talented."

"Really?" I light the cigarette and regret it. It's some Italian brand.

"But I suck."

"You suck at dancing. But you seem to…enjoy men."

"Well, do I have a choice?"

"You know what I mean. This is more than a job for you."

"Love your work and you'll never work a day in your life!" I laugh.

"That's why I want to talk to you. I think you should work at my other club. You'd make more money. You don't have to dance and the clients can take you home if they like you."

I know the place she's talking about. It's the place my ex took me. I still daydream about him daily. But I only have one fantasy: some unexpected night, he comes into my club. He pretends not to know me and buys a dance. He thinks he'll get to punish me. But inside those rooms I'm in charge. We do things differently. I suck all his power out through my pussy!

But that will never happen because he can't go to strip clubs anymore. Not seedy ones, at least. Fathers go somewhere fancy.

. . .

"I can't believe I'm going to have to use one of those." My ex points to a baby stroller. The passengers with babies always board first. We watch them from our seats at the gate.

"If the truth hurts, ignore it," I say smugly.

My ex and I are waiting on the flight from Linate to Orly. We are on our way to Paris. It's not a fantasy, it's not a daydream, it's not romantic. It's business.

"I'll carry the baby on my back like a monkey."

"Whatever you've gotta tell yourself, dude..."

The Banda is throwing a party in Paris for a new zine they made. They hired me to DJ. They said they miss their "Pupa." Yeah, I'd miss me too!

I couldn't say no—I owed Zina a visit! Plus, my ex said he'd pay for my ticket. And fly there with me. I haven't seen him since the...baby shower at PRAVDA.

My mom told me that after giving birth women forget the pain so that they can consider doing it again.

Women are built to omit catastrophes.

We met for breakfast at Gattullo. He looked the same. He ordered a brioche with cream and a cappuccino. I ordered a regular brioche and an Americano. He asked me how school is going. I said good. He asked me how work is going.

"How do you know about my work?"

"Tumblr."

I didn't know that perverted men with pregnant wives were allowed on Tumblr.

It was thrilling to know that he kept up with me. I didn't ask about him.

In the taxi to Linate he looked over at me and said, "your hair looks good."

"Platinum is a lifestyle." I shrugged.

"But you're too skinny," he said, and pinched my thigh.

"Thanks! Aren't I stunning?" I moved away from his grip and grinned.

That's the first time his opinion of me didn't shatter my opinion of myself.

I turned and looked out of the window. I felt drawn to him, but not magnetically. For once, he seemed more absorbed than me. I smiled to myself. Oh, what a few months can do! Some shift was taking place in the universe and it favored me.

In the car I decided to "play it cool" for the whole trip. Doing so is clearly working. Why have I never considered this trick before? Oh yeah, because before I was desperate, brain-dead, and out of touch. "Playing it cool" is one of the things I learned from Filip. Though I probably should have learned it in elementary school.

On the plane, I read a magazine and feel him looking me over. There's a lot to look at. I'm wearing: lacy pantyhose from Tezenis, silver platforms from Top Shop, short leather shorts from H&M, a black mesh leotard from American Apparel and my black fur coat from the market. I only brought my hideous purse as luggage: panties, tights, makeup, money, passport, cigarettes and condoms—*just in case.*

From Orly we head straight for a bar in Pigalle. I hope we'll have time for a drink, just us, but the Banda is already there. They order *frites, escargot,* and *fois gras.*

Pigs.

I order red wine. I listen to them talking about pornography and art and I wish they would leave us alone. My ex and I could start a new life here. I'd open a pigeon café (like a cat café but with pigeons) and he'd do...whatever it is he does.

But instead we go to the party. It's at a bar in Saint-Georges. Near Moulin Rouge. A bunch of people are here and I don't know any of them. We all have dinner downstairs at a big table. My ex orders everyone hamburgers without asking what they want first. It's sweet he's given me an excuse to not eat. There's a piano in the room. He says loudly, "Mia, play for us."

I say I can't.

He insists.

"Come on, Mia, you told me you played."

Everyone stares at me. I smile stupidly.

"I used to play but I don't remember anything."

"Nobody eats until Mia plays."

"Are you serious?" People put down their forks. Why is he doing this?

Everyone stares at me, as if they're kidnapped.

They're thinking, "play, putain, we're hungry."

I make my way to the piano and sit down. I close my eyes and try to recall the Moonlight Sonata. The only way to play a song you used to have memorized is to not allow yourself to actually think about the notes. The muscle memory in your hands must work on its own. I manage to play half a page and then my brain gets involved. I've forgotten it. I look up and laugh.

I announce: "I'm too drunk!"

Then I walk to the toilet.

In the hallway, a Terry Richardson impersonator takes my photos. The world is doomed if that's the kind of person people impersonate. I feel embarrassed for him, which eases my own embarrassment. He did me a kindness, unwillingly. I do what he wants, some basic "thumbs up" stuff, and head back to the table.

The mood changed after my piano failure so everyone's ready to go to the party.

It's upstairs in a creaky attic.

The "dance floor" is a bathroom. "So cool!" I hear someone say.

It's funny what people who have never been poor think is cool. Zina shows up with some girls. Before I can get to her she's taken by one of the Banda boys. He told me earlier that he would seduce my Russian friend. I told him she's used to royalty and war criminals, so he won't stand a chance. He said he'd pretend to have a wooden hand and that it "works every time."

I watch him introduce himself and explain why he can't shake her hand. He holds it up. It's covered by a black leather glove. He lets her touch it. Then he slams it on stool and she shrieks. She waves to me and points to him, like, "do you know this guy?" I wave back and give her a nod. I have no honor. I hear him tell her, "Just because I'm a pornographer doesn't mean I can't fall in love."

I forgot to bring my CDs. I'm playing the radio. Live performances are scheduled but I'm postponing them. I'm too protective of one of the acts. She's a chicken. This sleazy poet brought her here in a cardboard box. He says he'll read poetry with her. I don't trust him and I don't trust poetry. I'm not letting anyone touch her. I take off my top and hug her. Skin on skin contact is best. The poet pleads with me and promises to not hurt her. "She's my pet now."

As if being a pet means you won't get hurt.

After an hour or so Zina makes me let her go and "be social." I dance around on top of the sofa and fall into my ex's lap. I lay down with my head on his legs and he pets my hair. I roll over and look up at him. He looks down at me distantly. I want to tell him, "Let's get out of here" but before I can we get kicked out.

Everyone piles into cabs. I take a car with Zina and those girls. My ex gets in a car with his Banda. "Let's meet at Silencio!" the photographer yells at us.

At the club, I spot David Lynch and Lindsay Lohan—both are deflated in real life. After a couple hours, I realize my ex isn't coming. I tell Zina I want to go home. She brings the one-armed Banda boy with us. I reveal his secret and she goes to bed with him anyway. I don't blame her.

When the sun rises, I walk to Starbucks.

I order a black coffee and a muffin and text my ex.

"Hey where'd you end up?"

I finish my coffee and half of the muffin and text him again.

"Wanna have lunch?"

He doesn't answer.

24. MARRY THE NIGHT

December is so brutal I'm giving the pigeons pastries twice a day.

"Where are you going all dressed up?" the grey one missing an eye asks me.

"None of your business."

The park by Gattullo is bleak. Someone is asleep on the bench or maybe frozen to death.

My ex's baby is due soon. I bought a gift for...*it*. Because I'm mature, which is an adult word for "insane." It's a Disney music album.

Gotta get them cultured as early as possible.

We meet at Cape Town and have bloody mary's. I hand him the CD.

"That's so sweet of you," he says.

"Yeah, well."

He grabs my hand and holds it. "You look like you have three husbands."

I pull away in a futile act of self-preservation. Henry Rollins once wrote that women look their best in the cold. I think it's because men like the way women look when we're in pain.

I must be glowing.

"Yeah I'm really into wearing rings now." I put my hand back between my knees.

He smiles at my suffering and drinks his cocktail. He tells me the Bruttoposse party has changed locations. All the parties in town are moving or closing down. Maybe because I've stopped clubbing. Maybe because all these "party photographers" are killing the mystery. Ruining the whole point of parties, which is to disappear. Maybe because everyone prefers to stay home and blog.

Either way, the party only takes place once a month now. Downstairs in a bar next to Cape Town.

We finish our drinks and head in. He walks behind me. The room is sweaty and crowded. The people are the same people that went to Bruttoposse last year. This both disappoints and comforts me. He looks at me the way that he used to.

When I was a muse for sin.

We dance for a few songs and he pulls my top off. He likes to see other people look at me but only until I look back at them. Then he says we should leave. We're too horny to be in public and this is no swinger's club, after all.

I put my top on. I walk upstairs and he walks behind me, this time groping me.

I feel delirious and unable to control my actions. I'm a rat, headed for the poison. I hold onto him as we walk. We're headed in the same direction and when we reach the street where he's supposed to turn right and I'm supposed to go straight, he doesn't turn right. He stops and stands in front of me and pushes me against a wall. He kisses me hard. I feel his stubble grating my skin. He puts his hands down my pantyhose and unbuttons my leotard and shoves his fingers inside. He says, "I wanna fuck you."

"We can't here," I say.

"Where's your leash?" he asks, pulling me closer.

"By now? In a landfill in China."

He freezes. "What do you mean?"

I look down at the sidewalk and say, "I threw it away."

He takes his hand out of my tights and brings it under my chin. He lifts my face so I look up at him. He seems confused. Or hurt, if that's even possible.

"I left it in a trash can on Corso Italia."

"When?"

"Last spring. After I blocked you."

"Why?"

"Because it made me sad."

He hugs me and says, "Don't be sad. You'll always be my—"

"No, you don't get it!" I pull away before he can say the word.

"What?" he says, confused.

"It *always* made me sad." I'm surprised at the harshness of my voice.

He doesn't say anything, so I say I'm sorry. And he says it's OK. Though it should be him who says sorry. He turns around and he walks away, towards his home, where his wife is sleeping.

For once, I feel worse for her than for me.

As I walk home it starts to snow. It's hard to believe that the world keeps working when everything else is over. The snow doesn't give a damn about what shoes you're wearing or who's breaking your heart. I promise myself that this will be the last time I cry about him. Then I laugh out loud at myself for thinking a promise from me could mean anything.

My buzzer is buzzing. I open my eyes and reach for my Nokia. It's 8:00. Too early for Filip. I close my eyes again. The buzzing must be for my roommates. I get a text from Filip. "Open up, bitch!" The crazy tram lady must have chased him again. Or he's back from an after-party and locked himself out of his flat. Or he just robbed an AutoGrill and needs a hide-out. It could be anything with Filip.

I groan, roll out of bed and throw on my fur coat. My apartment is freezing.

I walk to the front door and buzz him up.

He arrives flustered. "I ran up the stairs," he pants. I ask why he didn't take the lift and he says, "It's too slow!" He's holding a pack of cigarettes, a box of Tavernello and his laptop under an arm.

"Filip it's so early." I say, trying not to sound annoyed.

Sleep has been elusive.

"It's out, Mia!" Filip is frantic. He seems possessed.

He's a pregnant woman whose water just broke in a taxi. He's a street dog sniffing out steak scraps in a dumpster. He's a pillhead who can't find their stash in a Prada hobo bag. Desperate!

He pushes past me and marches into my bedroom. He flops down on my bed, sits cross-legged and opens up his computer. "It's out and I need you with me."

"What's out?" I close the front door and rub my eyes. "I'll make some coffee," I yawn, heading for the kitchen.

"No, there's no time!" he screams.

"Come here! Sit down! NOW!"

My good looking roommate yells from his bedroom. *"SAI ZITTA!"*

"You shut up," I say under my breath. I go into my bedroom and shut the door. I sit down next to Filip. I cross my legs so our knees touch. He lights a cigarette, opens YouTube and says, "Are you ready?" I don't know what for. "Yeah," I say.

"I'm ready."

He presses play and goes, "Shhhhhhh."

I've neglected Lady Gaga ever since that concert last year. Even her new music stung me. This happens after any relationship. I can't listen to whatever an ex and I listened to together. In most cases, it hurts to recall the times we shared with the music. In Gaga's case, my ex didn't share her with me.

He stole her from me.

When I was really low a few days ago my friend Cat told me, "watch *Wild at Heart* and you'll remember who you are." I watched it and didn't like it. I figured she didn't really know who I am. This music video is doing what I think Cat wanted that movie to do for me. This music video is reminding me of everything. I am mine again. Lady Gaga is mine again. Or, I mean, I'm hers.

> *When I look back on my life,*
> *it's not that I don't want to see things exactly as they happened,*
> *it's just that I prefer to remember them in an artistic way.*
> *And truthfully, the lie of it all is much more honest.*
> *Because I invented it.*

Those are the opening lines. What follows them is astounding. *Marry the Night* is a masterpiece. Groundbreaking, revolutionary, iconic, legendary, gorgeous, brilliant, genius, chic, devastating and hilarious. It's more like a movie than a music video and more like a manifesto than a movie and more like a fashion film than anything else. Filip and I decide to watch the video all day, on repeat. "We have to skip class," he says. "And skip all our meals," I add.

We take the video through our routine. Today, our schedule is symbolic.

We watch it for hours in each location: my bedroom, California Bakery, campus, (no classrooms, just NABAR), and our bar in Col Di Lana. Neither of us have smartphones so we can't watch it while walking around. When we walk, we talk about the video. We stamp the images onto the map of our lives. The film's magic will stew in our usual chairs, stools, curbs, couches and pillows.

Each time we start fresh on the stark first scene, I feel

solace. So does Filip. I only take my eyes away from the nurses in "next season Calvin Klein" to study his face. He seems relaxed, for once. His features are soft. He's like a kid watching cartoons, completely immersed and vulnerable. He really is so young, I think. I guess that means I am, too. We don't have much but we've got so much time. And Tavernello.

Around midnight I walk home drunk and replay all the scenes in my head. My favorite is when she's in the mental hospital. And in the bath tub bleaching her hair. And dancing on cars, lit on fire. These scenes are to me what Bible Verses are to some people. *Marry the Night* is what I'll hold onto for strength and stability. It's what I'll look to for inspiration. It's the new standard I'll use to judge everyone and everything around me. I stumble around while humming the tune.

The dirty street rolls out in front of me and I smile.

Tonight is my birthday. I'm throwing a party in a Cuban bar in a dingy alley downtown. I didn't want to go to Cuore or any of those old places. The bartenders won't let me DJ. They're playing their Cuban music. Management will keep all the drink money I bring in.

I can hear my ex-boss in my head yelling, "Didn't you learn anything from me?"

I don't care, I just want to dance. Not for profit. I quit my job last night so I could be here. I was getting bored of it anyway. Maria is wearing a suit and looks like Diane Keaton in *Annie Hall*. Filip is wearing flesh-colored nylon stockings with blown-up balloons underneath. I'm wearing a sequined cocktail dress, Agent Provocateur lingerie (a gift from Zina) and Hello Kitty pasties, for when I inevitably take my top off.

This year I'll be a little older and a little more tasteful.

Zina came all the way from Paris for the weekend. I invited everyone! My good looking roommate is here and so is the regular looking one. The Banda is here. So are Flow,

Magro and Frank. The PRs are here and so are the journalists, fashion victims, crackheads, dealers, fakes, floozies, students and professors, even. My ex-boss couldn't make it but I really wish that she had. My ex did and I wish he hadn't.

"There's too many old people here," he says, looking around.

"Oh yeah? Then go home."

"Mia, stai bene?"

"I'm not here to *stare bene*."

I leave him at his table.

Zina and I dance on the bar. She even takes her top off. Filip blacks out in the bathroom. Maria flirts with my good looking roommate. It's nice to see her blushing.

My ex comes up to me and says, "come talk to me." I say, "give me one minute."

I go outside for a cigarette. I'm in just lingerie and my coat. I keep walking. I stop at a kebab place on Via Vigevano and order a vegetarian wrap. I sit on the curb and eat the whole thing, except for a scrap, which I throw to a pigeon. I haven't seen him in a while. He's rare, green and violet.

"How you doing baby?" I slur.

"Same old shit. You?"

"Same old shit."

The pigeon swallows and flies away. The words roll around my head.

Same old shit.

I smoke a cigarette and consider something.

I am not a pigeon. I stand up and walk to Porta Genova. There's a taxi stop by the trams. And I need to do something. It's my birthday and I deserve it.

I wrap the coat tight around me so it hides my underwear. Milanese taxi drivers are notoriously conservative. I tell the driver the address, which is seared into my memory. I pay him once we arrive, with a tip.

"Can you wait for me here?" I ask him.

"No," he says, and speeds off.

I'm at the entrance of the showroom I used to work at. Just seeing it gives me the chills. I turn my back to the door, take my underwear off and squat. I piss all over the entrance mat. *Benvenuti*, suckers.

I walk towards Porta Romana. There's a taxi stop at the station. I don't want to go back to my party. I wish there was a clean room somewhere for me. A bright space where nobody knows the taste of my spit. I can't go anywhere without seeing someone I've slept with, worked for or cried about. But I guess that's OK. It means I own this town, in some way. My sweaty hands have grabbed every surface. My feet have stomped down each block. My tears have closed all the parties.

I am my own party now.

ACKNOWLEDGMENTS

As a writer, I must thank Blogspot and Tumblr first. My sister, for insisting I start a blog all those years ago. My parents, for thinking everything I do is genius even if it makes them uncomfortable. My first editors, Tim Small, Lorenzo Mapelli and Daniele Cassandro. Alice Rossi, who translated my articles for years and helped me stay on schedule with this book. My husband Stefano, for supporting and loving me. Thanks for staying up with me those nights when I wrote until morning. Thanks for reminding me to eat. My dog Winkle, for taking me outside to play. Thanks to CLASH for believing in my story and guiding me through the publishing process. Thanks to the people who will recognize themselves in this book and to those who wonder why they aren't in it. Thanks to the pigeons, thanks to Milan.

Photo by Yulia Zinshtein

Tea Hacic-Vlahovic is a Croatian-American writer and performer. Previously a columnist for Vice and Wired Italy and contributing editor of Wonderland Magazine, she writes for the Columbia Journal, Dazed, Spike Art Magazine, Autre, and more. She's the founder of STAI ZITTA magazine and host of Troie Radicali podcast. She's the author of LIFE OF THE PARTY and A CIGARETTE LIT BACKWARDS. She lives in Los Angeles with her husband and their dog. Follow her on IG & Twitter @teahacic

ALSO BY CLASH BOOKS

TRAGEDY QUEENS: STORIES INSPIRED BY LANA DEL REY & SYLVIA PLATH

Edited by Leza Cantoral

GIRL LIKE A BOMB

Autumn Christian

99 POEMS TO CURE WHATEVER'S WRONG WITH YOU OR CREATE THE PROBLEMS YOU NEED

Sam Pink

THIS BOOK IS BROUGHT TO YOU BY MY STUDENT LOANS

Megan J. Kaleita

PAPI DOESN'T LOVE ME NO MORE

Anna Suarez

FOGHORN LEGHORN

Big Bruiser Dope Boy

TRY NOT TO THINK BAD THOUGHTS

Art by Matthew Revert

HEXIS

Charlene Elsby

THE ELVIS MACHINE

Kim Vodicka

WE PUT THE LIT IN LITERARY

CLASHBOOKS.COM

FOLLOW US

TWITTER

IG

FB

@clashbooks

PUBLICITY EMAIL

clashbookspublicity@gmail.com

CPSIA information can be obtained
at www.ICGtesting.com
Printed in the USA
JSHW021916240322
24173JS00005B/7